St. John and the Seven Veils

St. John and the Seven Veils

A DETECTIVE NOVEL

by William Babula

An Irma Heldman / Birch Lane Press Book
Published by Carol Publishing Group

A Birch Lane Press Book
Published by Carol Publishing Group
Birch Lane Press is a registered trademark of
Carol Communications, Inc.

Editorial Offices	Sales & Distribution Offices
600 Madison Avenue	120 Enterprise Avenue
New York, NY 10022	Secaucus, NJ 07094

In Canada: Musson Book Company
A division of General Publishing Co. Limited
Don Mills, Ontario

Manufactured in the United States of America
10 9 8 7 6 5 4 3 2 1

Carol Publishing Group books are available at special discounts
for bulk purchases, for sales promotions, fund raising, or
educational purposes. Special editions can also be created to
specifications. For details contact: Special Sales Department,
Carol Publishing Group, 120 Enterprise Ave., Secaucus, NJ 07094

Library of Congress Cataloging-in-Publication Data

Babula, William.
    St. John and the seven veils : a detective novel / by William
Babula.
        p.   cm.
    "An Irma Heldman/Birch Lane Press book."
    ISBN 1-55972-071-9
    I. Title. II. Saint John and the seven veils.
PS3552.A252S67   1991
813'.54—dc20   91-7570
                                                      CIP

For Karen,
As always

St. John and the Seven Veils

1

"I know who this man is, Mr. St. John," the woman sitting across from me said as she jabbed a police composite drawing in the newspaper with a carefully lacquered fingernail. We were using my beautiful partner Mickey's space because my desk in back was lost under a volcanic eruption of printouts; and Chief Moses, my other partner, a gigantic Seminole Indian whose wishes I usually respected, didn't like anyone messing up his carefully organized desk.

The woman handed me the *San Francisco Chronicle*. I took a long look at the drawing on the front page.

"I'm positive," the woman said.

I put the newspaper down. Why—since it was Saturday and the office was officially closed—had I let her in?

A P.I. shouldn't kid himself. I'd been taking a break from catch-up work in my apartment upstairs over the offices in the Stick-Eastlake style Victorian we rented when I saw her get out of a gold Mercedes sedan across the street. I opened up the office because I liked the way the lady looked getting out of that car.

Her name was Nancy Gutman. She was in her fifties but appeared to be a decade younger. Her hair was frosted but not brittle. She had blue eyes so large, the edges of the whites showed as sharp slivers above and below her irises. Her nose, above a delicate mouth, was perfect, thanks, I guessed, to a talented plastic surgeon. The skin at the corners of her eyes was stretched face-lift tight. Her lipstick and her fingernails matched a clinging red wool dress that did nothing to hide a figure a would-be starlet would kill for. She wore a double strand of pearls around her long, graceful neck. I found her to be a very classy work of art.

"Composite drawings can be misleading, Mrs. Gutman. There are so many variables," I said about the less-than-perfect work of art on the desk.

"Nancy." She smiled.

"Nancy," I said.

"I'm positive," Nancy repeated.

I picked up the police composite drawing and studied it again. When I put it down, I turned and stared out of the barred front window, the one with ST. JOHN DETECTIVE AGENCY lettered in gold on it.

It was an unusually warm April afternoon, consistent with the dry spring we had been having in San Francisco so far. The twin rows of plane trees lining Octavia Street were in new chartreuse leaf under a scoured blue sky. It was perfect for baseball, which had just begun its long season. The Giants were losing at a steady rate, but across the bay, the Oakland A's already looked like the team to beat in the American League.

I was working alone in the office while my partners spent the afternoon at the A's game, courtesy of a former client. This made me more than a little irritable, even though they had gone with my blessing—sort of. Mickey had always been a baseball fan and Chief Moses, who started with football (which he played briefly at Florida State) and had taken up playing basketball with me in the gym we built upstairs in my apartment, had recently gotten into baseball through some coed softball games he played in at San Francisco State.

Nancy shifted impatiently in her chair. She was used to being catered to. "Well?" she asked.

I didn't answer immediately.

This beautiful spring in the city, or "The City" as the local newspapers liked to glorify San Francisco, was being ruined by a series of apparently random murders, and one attempted murder, by a man the media were calling the April Fool Killer. This psycho started with a typed note to *The Chronicle* stating that his first victim (he had underlined *first*) would die on April 1. He signed it "April Fool." No one took it that seriously until a local business-man was killed—a knife thrust up through the rib cage and into the heart. It happened in his men's clothing store right after clos-ing Friday, April 1—Good Friday 1988. The police speculated the killer had hidden himself in a dressing room, waiting for the victim to be alone. He left "April Fool" written in blood on a glass display counter.

A week later a second note came, again signed "April Fool." The next victim would die April 11. A San Francisco attorney was mur-dered outside of his office the night of the eleventh. The same MO. The killer painted "April Fool" in blood on the attorney's new white BMW. Two days later a third note came to *The Chronicle* promising another death on April 17. Despite an increased police presence on the streets, a dermatologist was found knifed to death in his home on the seventeenth, "April Fool" in blood on the bed-room mirror.

Businessmen and professionals, a sizeable portion of the city's population, were panicked. The fourth note promised another death on April 21. The killer was batting a perfect 1.000 so far. On the twenty-first, just two days ago, he went after his second lawyer. Maybe he was a member of PAL—People Against Lawyers—who had gone berserk and branched out. I hoped he didn't have it in for private eyes as well.

The fourth target was Jacob Stein, an attorney who had a black belt in karate. Not a bad combination these days. Stein managed to disarm his attacker and get a good look at him before he got away. Because of the method of attack and the date, the police assumed Stein's assailant was the April Fool Killer. Police artists worked with Stein to put together the composite drawing.

It was this drawing that Nancy Gutman claimed to recognize. I read aloud: "He's approximately five ten and one hundred fifty pounds. Thin but very strong. Brown hair. Large blue eyes. A deep tan that doesn't hide two scars, one on the forehead, one on the neck."

"The description fits," she said as she took out a pack of Virginia Slims. "Do you mind?" she asked.

I pointed to the office sign. IF YOU MUST SMOKE, PLEASE DON'T

EXHALE. My two partners and I were all opposed to first and sec-
ondhand smoke and each of us had a sign at our desks.

"Seriously?"

"I'm allergic."

"To what?"

"Lung cancer."

"What kind of P.I. are you, anyway?"

"The kind that doesn't look for extra ways to die."

Nancy put the pack back into her purse. She toyed with her
pearls. She crossed her legs, made an ineffective tug to pull the
short skirt of her dress down, then reopened her purse. She
handed me a five-by-seven color photo of a young man of about
twenty.

The man in the photograph was anywhere from fifteen to twenty
years younger than the man in the police sketch. But despite the
age difference, there were similarities. The boy had long hair and
the man had a brush cut but both had a very pronounced widow's
peak. Both the boy and the man had a horizontal scar across the
middle of the forehead and a vertical scar down the left side of the
neck. The most striking similarity was in the division of the face
that both pictures showed. We all begin split in half in the womb,
and in the fusing of the two parts, marked by the two ridges under
our noses, we come together, but never exactly so. In this case, it
was less so than usual. The right side of the face was higher than
the left, with an arched eyebrow, an eye that angled upward, and a
half lip that turned up into a smile. The left side drooped with a
straight eyebrow, an eye that angled down, and a half lip that
snarled.

"They're the same person," she said. "See the two scars?"

"Yes. One across the forehead and one on the neck."

"He got the one on his forehead in a fishing accident," Nancy
said.

"And the other?"

"A bayonet wound. When he was in Vietnam."

I stood up. "Go to the police. This is multiple homicide we're
talking about."

I looked out the window again. Shadows were starting to
lengthen in the street. The beautiful day was winding down.

"No. I want client confidentiality." She swung one shoe recklessly from her toes.

"The courts and the police don't exactly smile on client-P.I. confidentiality. Not when anybody with enough money for some business cards can set up as one." I myself did have a board-certified license but I didn't bother to point that out. "Go see an attorney if you want confidentiality," I advised.

"You are an attorney as well as a private detective. That's why I came to you." She was staring at me intently with those enormous blue eyes. "That guarantees me confidentiality, doesn't it, Mr. St. John?"

I began to pace behind the desk. "I *was* an attorney. I saw enough in a D.A.'s office and in a private law firm to get out of the profession fast."

"I read about you in the newspapers six months ago when that actress was poisoned. I remembered that the stories said you were not only a detective but also an attorney."

"You've got a good memory."

"I'm not senile yet. In mind or body," she said, smiling.

"Not by a long shot. Either one." I sat down. "But I don't practice law anymore, Nancy."

"I don't care. It's confidentiality I want."

Nancy wasn't going to go away.

"All right. Who do you think this guy is?" I pushed the picture and the newspaper toward her. I had an idea, but I wasn't going to play guessing games.

She looked around. "Could you offer a lady a drink. Or is that out along with smoking?"

"I can only take this health bit so far." I got back up. "What would you like?"

"Do you have any vodka?"

One among many office improvements was a small refrigerator and a bar that we kept in the hallway outside of Chief Moses' middle office.

"Flavored or unflavored?" I asked.

"I'm impressed."

"You should be. This is a cut above cheap bourbon out of paper cups that you get from your typical gumshoe. It helps make up for the NO SMOKING signs."

"What flavors?" she asked.

"I've got Absolut Peppar from Sweden or Stolichnaya Limonaya."

"Limonaya. Is it chilled?"

"Of course."

"Then I'll have it straight up."

I took out the bottle of unopened Stoli and got two pony glasses from the bar. I filled them and went back into the office.

"Cheers," she said as she drank the Limonaya down in a single swallow.

"*Na zdorovye*," I said and matched her. I hadn't tasted the stuff before. It was smooth, with the flavor of a lemon drop.

Nancy got up and did a slow circle around the office. This was the windup. For the delivery, she said, "His name is Vincent. Vincent Gutman. The man in these pictures is my son."

Just what I had been afraid of.

"Nancy, I repeat, go to the police. I've got a friend in Homicide ... more or less..."

"No. I want you to find him before the police do. I have the money. My husband's death left me very well off."

So it was the window Gutman. I never doubted the money.

"It's not the money. It's the ethics involved. What if he kills again?"

"Before you can find him and stop him?"

"Yes." Here I was talking about stopping a psycho killer when I hadn't even taken the case yet. And knew I shouldn't.

"Since when are ethics part of the P.I. scene?"

"Sometimes you just trip over them in the dark. The practical problem is withholding evidence in a felony. We've got to go to the police."

"My, my, so righteous." She smiled. "I don't think you'll want to go to the police with my son's name."

"Why not?"

She paused for effect. "You see, Vincent Gutman is dead."

"That's a hell of a good reason."

Nancy sat down and raised her empty pony glass. I got her a refill, which she downed immediately.

"Tastes like lemon-drop candy," she said.

"About your dead son..."

She took out a letter and passed it over to me. It was on official-looking U.S. Army stationery. Corporal Vincent Scott Gutman was reported as missing during the North Vietnamese offensive of April 1972.

"It says that he's presumed dead."

"I have more. A death certificate." She handed a paper to me. "And I have a body. Vincent is buried in the Presidio cemetery."

"So I'm looking for a ghost?"

"Whatever your ethics can live with." She leaned back in the client's chair. The shoe she was dangling from her toes slipped off. Her toenails were painted the same vivid red as her lips and fingernails. "Will you do it?" she asked.

"Did you actually see the body before it was buried?"

"No. It was supposed to have been burned beyond recognition. The casket was sealed by the army."

"That casts some doubt on the ghost theory."

"Well?" she pressed.

I gave in and told her my fee.

"Fine. Promise you won't go to the police?"

"I'm not going to the cops with the information that a man who's been dead for sixteen years is the April Fool Killer. I've got to keep what little credibility I have with those guys intact."

"I thought you'd see it that way."

"So much for an ethical dilemma."

Nancy raised her empty glass.

"The stuff sneaks up on you," I warned as I went to turn on our new copy machine.

"Let it."

I made a copy of the story, the army letter, the death certificate, and a half dozen copies of just the composite drawing. When I was done I brought her another pony glass of Limonaya vodka. This time she only downed half of it with her first gulp. Her other shoe fell to the floor.

While she sipped the rest, I tried to find out everything I could about her son. She told me he had been married and had a daughter. His widow remarried, moved away, and cut off all contact. She had tried to find them but no luck. Nancy gave me the last known address and the woman's new name.

"What's her birth date?"

She gave it to me with the year and continued, "Vincent was just a kid when he got Barbara pregnant and they got married. He couldn't find a decent job, so he joined the army and kept reupping for Vietnam. He was on this third tour of duty when..."

I nodded. "You don't have to go into it."

"They had a beautiful daughter. Jacqueline. Jackie."

"So you haven't seen your granddaughter in years."

"I thought of hiring a private detective to track her down."

"I might have to."

"It would be wonderful to see her again."

"How old would she be now?"

"Twenty-one..." Her voice trailed off.

The vodka and the emotion caught up with Nancy. She passed out. She spent the twilight lying on the old couch in my office while I made an attempt to finish up my work for a jury-research firm that the attorneys Forsander and Samaho had set us up with. After the Cole case that caught Nancy's attention they had kept their promise to keep sending work our way. The jury-research firm employed us to investigate the pool of prospective jurors, determining age, occupation, race, sexual orientation, religion, and political party. We also took photos of the houses they lived in and the cars they drove. After that, our work was done. The firm then employed a crew of psychologists to interpret the data and root out unfavorably disposed jurors. It didn't give you great faith in the jury-selection system, but with two hundred jurors in a pool, my partners and I were kept busy and well paid.

I put the last pieces of data into my new Mac and set it to PRINT.

The agency had been doing so well over the winter that we now each had a Mac. The old electric typewriters were gone. We were high tech. We also used our profits to secure the office. We not only had a video scanner for the porch, we also had a computerized combination digital alarm and lock with a numerical sequence for the front door, and bars on all of the first-floor windows. The wrought-iron bars were the kind that could be unlocked and swung open in case of a fire. Too many people had burned to death locked in by their own security.

I stacked up the printouts together with the car and house pictures I'd had developed at the Quick-Pics photo shop. Finally the job was done. I could see the surface of my desk again.

The phone rang without waking Nancy. It was Tommy Dong, a third generation Vietnamese-American, a friend of the Chief's and a former client. The problem we thought we had solved for Tommy was surfacing again. I promised him that Chief Moses would get back to him as soon as possible.

I called a messenger service to pick up the reports. The consulting firm never closed down.

I made some coffee in our Mr. Coffee machine and got Nancy up. She looked even younger in her sleepy, disheveled state. She drank the coffee, eyeing me sheepishly over the rim of the cup.

"I drank too much too quickly," she said.

"It happens to all of us."

"I'd better be getting home."

"You sure you can drive?"

"No. I better not."

I called a cab.

While we waited I asked the key question: "If your son is alive, where has he been all of these years?"

"I don't know," she said, averting her eyes.

I had an idea but I wasn't ready to dig into it yet. Not until I dealt with the primary business at hand.

"First I find out if he's really alive," I said.

"He is. I know it. And thank you, Mr. St. John," she said and kissed me. It was close to a motherly peck. But not quite. The cabbie was impatiently blowing his horn. We ignored him. "I don't usually drink like that," she added.

"You have to watch out for lemon drops. And call me Jeremiah."

She gave me her address, phone number, and a check as an advance payment.

Ten minutes after she left, the messenger arrived—a young black man in uniform with an M shaved on each side of his head—and I gave him my package. I was meeting my partners at six o'clock at one of our favorite restaurants. They'd tell me all about the game I missed. Try to rub it in.

I had a few things to tell them myself.

2

I had been waiting for my partners for nearly an hour at the Hyde Street Grille, a clean no-frills place with bare, whitewashed walls and plain storefront windows. Three printed menus, a recent innovation at the Grille, lay closed on the Formica table. I was nursing my third Henry Weinhard's when Mickey showed up.

"It was a great game. Jose Canseco hit one into the left-field bleachers," she said as she pulled out a chair and sat down. She was dressed in a tight yellow sweater and green slacks, the A's colors— which she liked because they went well with her honey-blond hair and green eyes. I liked what she was wearing because it also went well with a five-eight figure that had all of the right curves. And I wasn't thinking pitching.

"You were supposed to be here at six," I said.

"A truck dropped a load of processed fish parts on the Bay Bridge. The traffic was incredible. And so was the smell."

"How about the catch of the day for dinner?"

She grimaced. Even that looked good on her.

Michelle "Mickey" Farabaugh joined my agency after some time on an Ohio city police force. When she appeared nude in a *Playboy* "Women in Blue" pictorial, that time was over. I got her on the rebound.

"Where's the Chief?" I asked.

"He hunts for the last parking space left by white men in the city," Mickey explained, imitating the Chief's Indian-reservation English. The Chief could shift his language from standard English to movie Indian whenever the occasion warranted it.

Knowing the way Chief Moses handled his pickup truck, I felt sorry for the owners of any cars he decided to squeeze between.

Mickey ordered a half carafe of the house white.

"How did Pete do?" I asked.

Mickey and the Chief handled Pete's case and Pete had given them box seats to today's game against the White Sox as a bonus. Pete was a young ballplayer who had come to us for help because he was being hassled by a sports agent who had threatened to have Pete's kneecaps broken if he didn't sign with him. The situation was complicated because Pete had accepted small amounts of money from the agent while he was playing ball for Stanford. A clear violation of NCAA rules. But the agent didn't exactly hold the moral high ground.

Standard St. John Agency procedure in this kind of situation is to get more on the bastard than he has on the client. Mickey and Chief Moses got enough dirt on the agent to drive him out of the Bay Area. He quickly set up business in L.A. but that wasn't our problem. In the City of Angels he'd fit right in, anyway.

"All he did was sit on the bench," Mickey said.

"At least it wasn't because he had broken knees."

"Too bad you couldn't come."

"This was your case and the Chief's. And I made the commitment on those juror reports." I sounded more magnanimous than I felt.

"That's true."

I took a sip of beer. The bottle wasn't as full as I had thought.

I had started on another by the time Chief Moses—splendid in a silky green and gold A's warmup jacket and matching cap—arrived. The jacket must have been double extra large to fit the Chief's six-foot-seven nearly three-hundred-pound body—almost all of which was muscle.

He took off the cap, shook out his mane of black hair, and sat down.

"Trouble parking?" I asked.

"I had to park on the sidewalk."

"Good luck with the parking patrol," I said.

"That is where the cops park." The Chief ordered a Bud.

I didn't want to discuss the odds on his getting a ticket or towed. So I asked, "Enjoy the game?"

"Yes. Jose Canseco hit a home run."

"That happens once in a while."

"I am a fan of Canseco." He swallowed down half of his beer. "He, too, is from Miami."

The Chief was a mixture of bloodlines that he simplified to Seminole. He was from a South Florida Indian village that he simplified to Miami. After wrestling gators for tourists in the Everglades, he spent time in L.A. as a mechanic and then moved on to be a bouncer in Vegas—among other things. Before he joined the agency, he was doing consulting for Indian tribes setting up Bingo games on their reservations.

"Can we order dinner? I've got a date tonight," Mickey said.

"With that doctor?" I asked.

"Yes."

Mickey's dating continued to grate on me. Briefly on we had been lovers but Mickey broke it off. Too much of a complication when you're partners in a business, she insisted. Complication or not, I was still more than a little in love with her.

"Is this the TV Medicine Man?" the Chief asked.

"Yes. And he has a name. Dr. Glenn Earnhard. Now can we order?"

"Sure. I wouldn't want you to be late."

I didn't like the TV doctor and not just because he was dating Mickey. He was central-casting handsome and came off like a snake-oil salesman with his superficial discussions of treatments for distressed-bowel syndrome, fibroid breast lumps, male hair loss, impotence, infertility, and everything else you didn't want to hear about on the evening news. Plus his personal life was a disaster. He had just divorced his fourth wife amid a lot of lurid publicity. He wasn't exactly the kind of doctor mothers were always trying to find for their daughters. Also, I suspected that his thick head of hair wasn't really growing out of his scalp. Small consolation.

I signaled to our waitress, a young Indian woman with a red jewel in her forehead. She was holding a chalkboard of specials.

"They'd like the fish," I said.

"You heard about the spill," the Chief noted.

"Mickey mentioned it."

"Scratch the fish," Mickey said. "And don't you dare order it, Jeremiah. I'll go sit at another table if you do."

The Chief ordered one of the large specialty hamburgers with everything but onions.

"No onions?" I asked.

"It is jersey night."

This meant that the Chief had a Florida State football jersey picked out for his date. The jerseys had a Seminole head on the front—which resembled the Chief—and different numbers on the back to help him keep his ladies straight. He called them party favors, which had some truth to it.

Mickey, as usual, was on a diet. She ordered something called Pakistani diet chicken plate.

I ordered chicken curry with garlic fruit sauce. "Make that extra heavy on the garlic," I said. I wouldn't be kissing anyone tonight.

"How was your day, Jeremiah?" Chief Moses asked.

"I was waiting for someone to ask."

"Don't be so shy," Mickey said.

"We had a call from Tommy Dong. There's been another threat to one of his poker parlors."

"I was sure that case was closed," Chief Moses said.

The Chief knew Tommy Dong from Nevada. Tommy had shifted from Vegas to Tahoe and now ran a string of legal poker parlors in Northern California.

"Look into it, Chief."

"I will talk to the Yellow Suns. Again."

We thought the problem had been solved when Tran Van Dam, the head of a Vietnamese gang called the Yellow Suns, admitted— under the kind of duress the police don't have as a legal option— that they were trying to extort money from Tommy's operation. The leader understood that further attempts at extortion would have serious and painful consequences. The Yellow Suns were not heard from since. We hoped they had set for good.

Our food came. We ate quickly in silence.

"Anything else?" Mickey asked as she pushed her half-eaten chicken away.

The Chief and I looked down at our empty plates and ordered two more beers.

"A new client walked in off the street."

"What kind of case?" Mickey asked.

"Missing person. Sort of."

"A case for the Great Tracker?" Chief Moses asked. He liked hunting down missing persons. His specialty was lost children. The Chief had a high success rate with missing kids.

"What do you mean, Sort of ? Is this one of your charity cases?" Mickey had the rock heart of the real businesswoman—at least when it came to bottom lines.

"No. That's not it. There are complications. The police are looking for him, too."

"Why?" she asked.

I filled them in on the details of my meeting with Nancy Gutman.

"So she believes that her son, supposedly killed in Vietnam and buried in the Presidio, is alive and the April Fool Killer," Mickey whispered.

"What are we doing looking for him? That is police work, Jeremiah," the Chief said.

I swallowed some beer. "It depends. Right now Gutman is officially dead. Do we bring that to the cops?"

"This is withholding evidence in a felony," Mickey said.

"What evidence? The word of a distraught woman who wants her son to be alive?"

"So you think Gutman is really dead?" the Chief asked.

"Chances are good."

"What if he beat the odds. What if we find out he's alive?" Mickey asked.

"The army identified the body," I said.

"I'm supposed to find that reassuring? What if the army is wrong and this Mrs. Gutman is right?" she continued.

"Then we have a problem," I admitted.

"So we go to the police now," Mickey said.

"You're not a cop anymore," I reminded her. "We have clients not perps. I promised this client I wouldn't go to the police yet."

Mickey pushed her chair back. "I don't like it. I'm also late. So I am out of here."

As Mickey started for the door, I said, "He did a dermatologist. I'd tell your TV doctor to be careful."

"You be careful, Jeremiah, or we'll be visiting you in jail. So stuff it," she said as she went out the door.

"I guess she means the check," I said.

"Mickey is right about the police."

"The woman came to me because she knew I was an attorney. For now we're claiming attorney-client confidentiality."

"This Gutman case is bad medicine," the Chief said with a straight face. Those were his last words of wisdom before he too departed for his date.

I knew he was right. I knew Mickey was right. What we had to do was get some actual physical evidence that Gutman was alive— and damned fast!

I felt very alone. There were at least two women I could call who just might be free. Except it was Mickey I wanted to be with. I ordered a final Henry Weinhard's to wash everything away.

It didn't work.

The waitress brought me the check on a small plastic tray.

I put my credit card on the tray and the card and the check disappeared immediately. There were people lined up outside waiting to get in. As I watched the waitress hurry back toward me, I realized that neither Mickey nor the Chief had told me who won the A's game.

3

I waited until ten Sunday morning, which I thought was a reasonable enough hour, and called Mickey.

"This better be important, Jeremiah," she complained. "You woke me up."

"You shouldn't let the TV doctor keep you up so late. Or did I wake him, too?"

She hung up.

I called back. "Can I start over?" I asked.

"One chance."

"I'll be over in twenty minutes."

"Drop dead."

"Make that thirty minutes."

"Why?"

"We've got some investigating to do regarding Vincent Gutman."

"On Sunday morning?"

"It's the best time for all kinds of things, including..."

"Cool it, Jeremiah. Be over here in forty-five minutes. I'm a mess." She hung up again.

I called back.

"What now?"

"Wear a business suit."

She mumbled something and hung up once again.

I put on dark cotton slacks, a pale blue button-down shirt, a yellow and blue paisley tie, and a dark blue blazer that hid my shoulder holster with its walnut-handled Smith & Wesson .38 automatic. I slipped into black tasseled loafers.

I put some copies of the composite drawing into my inside jacket pocket.

I thought about calling the Chief but decided against it. The three of us didn't fit very well in my '56 Thunderbird coupe and I didn't feel like hearing more complaints about it. Besides, I felt Mickey and I could handle what I had in mind.

I went downstairs to my desk and got the business card I wanted. It was part of a collection I'd amassed over the years. In this racket, you never can tell who you'll need to impersonate to crack a case—from chiropractor to exterminator. In one case, in order to search a house, we convinced a family to move out because we had to tent the structure to kill a termite infestation. They went to a motel for two days and we found what we were looking for. In another case, after Dr. Moses did some chiropractic muscle and bone manipulations, we got the information we needed from the patient. All it took were the right business cards.

I set myself to the task of programming the digital alarm and lock that protected the office. With that done, I shut the invulnerable door and stepped out into a cool morning. Nancy's Mercedes was still parked across the street.

My car was down on Sutter, two blocks away. It stood under a sign that allowed only two-hour parking during the day unless you were an area resident with a "G" permit. I waived my distaste for bumper stickers and displayed the "G" decal for parking survival.

I drove over to Mickey's high-rise apartment on the Embarcadero north of the Ferry Building and parked in a loading zone. It had been forty-five minutes since I spoke to her. When she didn't appear in five, I hit the horn steadily enough to be a nuisance to the neighborhood. Ten minutes later Mickey appeared.

"Goddamn that horn!" she said as she got in.

"It took you an hour."

"I told you I was a mess."

I looked her over without my usual subtlety. "What the hell. It was worth the wait."

"Sure," she said.

"I mean it."

"She wore her man-tailored business suit with black textured stockings and black sling-back high heels. The effect was very sexy.

"Ow," she said as she tried to get comfortable on the bench seat—in '56, Ford had not yet gone to bucket seats.

"What's the matter?"

"I'm sore."

I pulled away from the curb. "I won't ask you where."

"All over," she said and grinned.

"Must have been some night."

"We went to his tennis club and played mixed doubles for three hours."

"How's the good doctor at tennis?" I asked.

"Glenn is very good," she said.

I stopped at a red light. Tennis was a sport I had played before my basketball obsession. I knew Mickey played a little but this was the first I had heard about Earnhard. I felt a macho confrontation crackling in the air. A match for the love of the lady. But first I had to recover my game. Something that always takes longer than you expect.

Mickey readjusted herself. "Where are we going?" she asked. "I hope this isn't going to be a long ride."

"To find Vincent Gutman."

"What's the reason I had to dress like this?"

"We've got roles to play. And we both need to look our parts." I handed her the business card I had selected.

She looked at it quizzically. "What's this going to do?"

I explained my plan to her. She was skeptical.

"Do you have a better idea?" I asked.

"If we need it. What's first?"

"A visit to the cemetery."

I continued through light traffic along the Embarcadero, past the working piers, and past Pier 39, a pier gone shopping mall, and the ever-crowded Fisherman's Wharf. I went past Aquatic Park, The Cannery, Ghirardelli Square, and the Fort Mason Center— which now housed every avant-garde literary group and art group and environmental group in the city.

"I feel like a tourist," Mickey said.

We drove along Marina Boulevard, between yacht harbors and a park filled with kids flying kites to our right and on our left the small mansions built on the landfill of the Marina District. In a big quake the land below us would turn to Jell-O and the mansions would come crashing down. But the low percentage of homes that were covered by earthquake insurance in the area made it clear that in 1988 most people were not worried about a repeat of the 1906 disaster.

I turned up Broderick to Lombard and drove through the entrance gate to the Presidio.

The Presidio is the headquarters of the Sixth U.S. Army. It was built by a Spaniard from Mexico in 1776. The Spaniard had chosen well. The base is set on fifteen hundred acres of prime tree-covered, bay-view real estate. If the army ever leaves the Presidio, it is slated by law to become a part of the national park system. It has a semiprivate entrance onto the Golden Gate Bridge, which despairing developers have been known to jump from after riding through the untouchable Presidio.

I drove along the hilly curves, past white stucco buildings with red tile roofs, past the large wooden homes of the officers, to the National Cemetery, slope after slope of grass and marble looking out over Doyle Drive and San Francisco Bay.

We passed through the open iron gate and parked by the cemetery administration building. Behind it were a few maintenance buildings of the same stucco and red tile. In front of the main building a black Chevy Citation was parked—the kind of car GM no longer produces. That seemed appropriate. It had official army plates and GOLDEN GATE NATIONAL CEMETERY lettered on its sides.

"Step one in the investigation," I said as I led Mickey away from the T-Bird.

We were standing in a road across from seven rows of identically shaped tombstones set down on a field of light green grass that looked in need of water. Our beautiful dry spring days meant the threat of drought and the imposition of watering restrictions. Above the grave markers was a road lined with eucalyptus trees. The road went on to wind up a hill to the highest point in the cemetery.

At the top of that hill I saw something moving. It took me a few moments before I realized it was a jogger in a pink running suit. From this distance he looked like a brightly colored jelly bean rolling down toward us. I knew that joggers ran everywhere through the city, but turning the Presidio cemetery into a fitness trail seemed like desecration.

"That sucks."

Mickey looked in his direction and scowled in agreement.

"How do we find the right tombstone?" she asked as she turned back toward me.

I pointed to a small ground marker by the curb that read SEC-TION H. "Mrs. Gutman told me how to find it."

We started to walk through the tablet-shaped tombstones, each of which looked like half of the ten commandments. Behind the burial field was a stand of Monterey cypress. At its edge was a white flagpole with an American flag waving in a light breeze. Behind it stood a large white marble monument hung with a red wreath. It looked like a tomb of an unknown soldier.

Five markers down the center column we found it. There was a cross in a circle at the top of the tablet of stone. Under the cross was carved:

IN MEMORY OF
VINCENT
SCOTT
GUTMAN
CORPORAL
U.S. ARMY
VIETNAM

According to the tombstone, Vincent Gutman died in Vietnam on April 11, 1972.

A visit to a military garden of stone always moves me. In another cemetery under another stone tablet lies Sergeant David St. John with the place-name Korea.

"You look upset," Mickey said.

"My father is buried under one of these in D.C."

"I didn't know."

"He died during a truce violation by the North Koreans three years after the war ended. He was just twenty-two. A kid."

"Did he ever see you?"

"Once. When I was a few months old."

"That's sad, Jeremiah."

"I understand Nancy Gutman. My mother told me that at first she didn't believe he was really buried there. She told me she spent those first years thinking he would just walk in the door one day."

I didn't like to talk about it. Or much else in that part of my life. That was one legitimate complaint that Mickey had about me.

But she didn't mention it today. Instead, she took my hand. I blinked my eyes and turned away from Gutman's grave and Vietnam. The war that could have been mine except for the death of David St. John in Korea. As I approached draft age during the Vietnam War, I learned that by law sole surviving sons were not drafted. Some guys have all the luck. Instead of going off to war, I went to college and studied acting and drama—the best preparation for the law. And not bad for P.I. work, either.

Still holding hands, we walked back to my black T-Bird.

The jelly bean jogger had finally puffed his way down the road to Section H. Above his pink velour suit and matching running shoes, the man's heavy face was a clashing bright red. His pained breathing broke the silence of the dead.

As he came up to us I said, just loud enough for him to hear, "You ought to haul your fat ass out of here and jog on 101." That was like telling your kids to go play in the street.

He slowed down and shot us a bird.

"Nice gesture," I said and started after him.

For a fat man, he could move when he had to.

I stopped and pulled out my S&W and aimed it in his direction.

"Jeremiah!" Mickey shouted.

I yelled to the pink jelly bean. "I'm an undercover MP and jogging is prohibited in the cemetery. You run through here again and I'll blow your balls off. If you've got any."

The fat jogger made it out of the gate with his life and his balls intact.

"He's the kind of guy who would report this," Mickey warned.

I holstered my gun. "Why? I said I was an MP."

"Right. And I'm Joan of Arc. Let's get out of here."

I went out through a different exit, passing by larger sandstone and marble monuments from earlier wars as well as more of the endless tombstone columns marching off to their vanishing point.

We drove back through the base, past white stucco Spanish-style barracks.

"So we found the tombstone," Mickey said.

"Now we find out about the remains buried under it," I said as I pulled into the circle in front of Letterman Army Medical Center.

4

Letterman Hospital rose eight sandstone stories into a cobalt sky. The architecture was pure army. The facade undulated like a vertical sheet of corrugated metal resting on top of four spear-shaped columns.

A medical supply truck was parked in the loading zone. Two patients in khaki robes were sitting on the sidewalk playing cards with their backs to the building, soaking up the warm sunshine.

I gestured toward the building. "I'd try to escape, too."

I decided not to challenge the Military Parking Police and drove out of the circle. I swung down behind the building and parked in a visitor's space in the lot.

We got out of the car and started up a steep path.

"I still don't know why you think the lab will be open on Sunday," Mickey said.

"I told you. This is an army base. Our national defense never rests."

We walked past the card-playing patients into the lobby. There were a few metal chairs standing on a cold tile floor. The greenish walls were bare except for a hospital directory. I went over to the information desk and flashed my business card at the woman in charge. The card identified me as an insurance company representative. She put down the Sunday comics and looked at it.

She was wearing a green WAC uniform with a nameplate that read Pvt. Craig. She was thirtyish, stocky, and had her hair cut so short, it looked like a crewcut. But she had a pretty, round face and eyes the color of chocolate kisses. Except for some lipstick, she wore no makeup.

I smiled at her.

"So?" she said to my smile and the card. "I don't need life insurance."

"I'm not selling life insurance. I'm a death claims investigator."

She stared at me. "It doesn't say that on your card."

"It's considered in poor taste," I explained.

"What do you want here?" she asked curtly.

"We need to talk to someone in charge of identifying MIA's. A question has been raised about a certain set of remains."

She looked at us as if we were ghouls come to rob a grave. "And the insurance company doesn't want to pay off?"

"We're just doing our job," I said.

"I'm just doing mine. Dr. Koyota said no visitors today."

Mickey stepped in. "We're not authorized to discuss our real purpose except with the person directly involved."

"Discuss it with me or forget it," Private Craig said.

Mickey sighed, delved into her handbag, and gave her a business card. "It's what we're really here for," she explained. "But you've got to keep it absolutely secret. If security is breached, we can't use the individual."

Private Craig read it, gave me a scornful look, and actually smiled at Mickey and said, "I understand. Usually I'd make an appointment for you during the week. But the doctor loves publicity." In less than a minute she was on the phone calling upstairs. We overheard her say that she was sending up two visitors and that he would be pleasantly surprised. Mickey put her forefinger to her lips and warned her to silence. "That's all I can tell you," Private Craig said.

After the call, we were wearing visitor badges on our lapels and riding an elevator up to see Dr. Elgin Koyota, the Scientific Director of the West Coast Branch of the U.S. Army Identification Lab, and a man, according to Private Craig, who was there night and day eight days a week.

"What card did you give our WAC friend to get us up here?"
"The right stuff."
"Which was?"
"It's a secret. Which she better keep."
"Come on," I said.
"Later, Jeremiah."
The elevator passed another floor on its slow rise.
"Dr. Elgin Koyota in charge of identifying American remains? I thought we all looked alike to Orientals," I said.
Mickey punched my arm as the elevator doors opened.
The lab was right across from us. In front of its pebbled glass double doors stood Dr. Elgin Koyota, identified for us by a small nameplate pinned to the breast pocket of his white smock. He was tall for a Japanese. He had black hair in a brush cut over a high forehead and hard dark eyes. He looked like he was in his twenties, although I knew he had to be older.
We exchanged introductions and shook hands. He had a firm grip and an eye for Mickey's legs.
I started toward the lab door but Koyota signaled for me to halt.
"You have a visitor's badge. It does not give you security clearance for the lab area." Like his grip, his voice was firm.
"What's in there?" I asked.
"It is classified. Please come this way."
Koyota led us down the antiseptic hallway to a private office. It was small, windowless, and carpetless. Against one wall stood a glass-enclosed display case that held a collection of skulls. Each was tagged. I noted an Africanus, an Erectus, a Neanderthal, a Cro-Magnon, and a Sapiens. A full skeleton hung in a corner in front of an anatomical chart. I wondered how his house was decorated.
Mickey and I each took a metal chair across from what looked like a human skull on Koyota's matching metal desk. In the middle of the desk, behind the skull, was an IBM PC.
"What can I do for you?" he asked. He was smiling, expecting to be pleasantly surprised, as Private Craig had promised.
I looked at Mickey but she didn't give me a clue. I started the insurance routine again.
Dr. Koyota looked puzzled. "Are you with death claims, too?" he asked Mickey.

Mickey nodded.

"I am going to have to have a litle talk with Private Craig," he said.

"Why?" I asked.

"She seems confused about who you are," he said. His tone implied that we had something to do with this confusion.

"An innocent misunderstanding," Mickey assured him. " We can only give details to individuals directly involved in the case."

Mickey, whose skirt was hiked up enough to reveal some black-stockinged thigh, leaned forward and pinned Koyota with her eyes.

He tried to keep his eyes on her face. He failed. A real leg man.

"What exactly are you after, Ms. Farabaugh?" he asked, acting like I had disappeared from the room.

"It has to do with some reporting technicalities. We don't expect to recover anything we paid out. But we do like to have our records accurate," she explained.

"What we're talking about, Doctor, is the basis upon which a Corporal Vincent Gutman's identification was made." I gave him the details I had about Gutman.

"I will have to get his file." Elgin Koyota excused himself and left us alone in his office.

I winked at Mickey.

She pushed back a wave of hair from her forehead and winked back.

This is when the TV gumshoe starts going through everything in the office and discovers whatever was missing to break the case. I just took a few business cards from Koyota's desk instead.

He came back carrying a plain gray file folder and spread it open on the desk.

"I thought all of this would be computerized," I said.

Koyota sat down. "Not for someone identified in 1972." He began to sift through the file.

"How are the remains usually identified?" I asked.

He looked up. "To date 248 sets of remains have been indisputably identified. In most of these, the teeth are recovered and matched with dental records. In fact, for the 2,394 American military personnel still listed as missing, dental records have been computerized for access and comparisons." He tapped on the PC.

"Was Gutman identified through his dental records?" Mickey asked.

Koyota was turning pages. "Apparently not."

"Why not?" I asked.

"It says that the dental records were not adequate to confirm the identification. That could mean anything. Dental records get destroyed in fires. Or your dentist dies. The files get lost somewhere. Then there's a lack of X-rays. Who knows?"

He flipped another page.

"And the victim's teeth were badly damaged, I see."

"Then this identification is not exactly indisputable," I noted.

"These days we have everything," Koyota said. "Now we can work with DNA analysis, creating a genetic blueprint. But back then, without adequate dental records, we used all other available information: age, race, height, bone structure, available medical X-rays, and details of the incident itself."

"In Gutman's case?" I asked.

Elgin Koyota shifted his eyes to me. "Apparently through accounts of the incident itself."

"What kind of incident?" Mickey asked.

"American planes inadvertently bombed their own positions during a North Vietnamese attack."

"Were all the soldiers accounted for?" she asked.

He sat there reading for several minutes. "No. There were MIA's never accounted for in that action."

"They could have been captured," I said.

"It is possible." He turned and showed us his left profile. "Do either of you smoke?" he asked.

"No," I answered.

"I thought you couldn't smoke in a hospital," Mickey said. "Isn't there a law against it?"

He nodded. "Never mind. I am trying to break the habit anyway."

Mickey looked at the skulls. "Good idea."

"Dr. Koyota, would you accept the Gutman identification today?" I asked.

As he reached around the IBM and picked up the skull on his desk, I thought of Hamlet in the gravedigger's scene. Koyota did his own bit of posturing.

"Off the record, it would not be indisputable. But I would not be willing to testify in court to that."

"Then the man buried in the Presidio cemetery may not be Vincent Gutman," I said.

Koyota closed the file. "Or he very well may be. There is compelling circumstantial evidence that he is."

"But not compelling scientific evidence," I said as I got up.

"No," Koyota agreed.

"Thank you, Dr. Koyota," Mickey said, "you've been very helpful."

We walked down the hall and left him standing in front of the lab. He bowed his head at us as we got into the elevator.

"He seemed taken with you," I noted after the doors closed.

"Must have liked my bone structure."

"What is it with you and doctors anyway?"

I didn't get an answer.

We went outside into the bright sunlight. The two card-playing patients were gone.

"So now, tell me what kind of business card you handed her?"

Mickey grinned and gave me one. It said that she was a producer for the new TV show.

"Jesus Christ!"

"First chance I've had to use it."

"Worked better than mine."

"Good thing," she said.

"Good thing he had an eye for your thigh bones," I said.

"What now?" Mickey asked as we got into the car.

"Lunch," I offered.

Mickey, who was always up for lunch, said, "I lost my appetite in there."

We decided to skip lunch.

I drove to a new Union 76 station where there were no attendants, just a cashier in a glass booth who took your cash or your credit card. While Mickey filled the tank at the orange and blue self-serve pump, I called Nancy Gutman from a pay phone back by the locked rest rooms that you needed a quarter to use. The sign said that they made change for the johns at the cashier's booth. Some operation.

"Your son may be alive," I said when she answered the phone.

"I know that."

"If there's another threat, I'm going to have to go to the police."

There was a long silence. "Find him first, Jeremiah, please."

"I'll try." I hung up.

When I got back into the T-Bird, Mickey said, "If we had a cellular car phone, we wouldn't have to look for phone booths."

"We needed gas."

"This time."

"Add it to the high-tech list." It was the list Mickey the expert was in charge of. She expanded it almost weekly.

Mickey grinned. I drove off in the direction of the Tenderloin. There was a man we had to see about a war.

5

A few years ago I wouldn't have driven my car into the Tenderloin. A few years before that I wouldn't have gone into the Tenderloin on a bet. Back then the area north of Market at the base of Nob Hill was dubbed by a local newspaper "Hell at Your Doorstep." It was like Nob Hill rolled its garbage down Leavenworth Street and where it stopped was the Tenderloin. Back then the area belonged to the pimps, whores, smut dealers, and drug dealers. They were the retail economy. Senior citizens locked themselves in their cold one-room apartments, afraid to go out to the one grocery store in the district on Geary—where the prices were too high anyway. "Hell at Your Doorstep" had the highest crime rate in the city. It had 25 percent of all homicides and 40 percent of all drug overdoses.

City Hall's plan for the area was simple: Bulldoze it in preparation for gentrification. This plan aroused the soon-to-be-homeless citizens. It wasn't Pacific Heights but it was the only place in the city they could afford to live. A coalition of whites, blacks, and the new Southeast Asian refugees fought back by transforming the Tenderloin from the inside out. The bulldozers never came.

I drove down Van Ness and turned east on Eddy Street. Once almost all of the storefronts here were boarded up. Now there were over a thousand businesses in forty square blocks, from a

Folk Showplace music shop on Turk and Original Joe's restaurant on Taylor to used-book stores and Asian video-rental shops. And of course the grocery stores. There were crowded groceries selling fresh produce, flowers, meat, poultry, and fish on every block.

We passed Battambang Market, the first Cambodian grocery in the Tenderloin.

"I think there are more groceries here than anywhere else in the city," Mickey said.

"Asian entrepreneurs. They're saving this place."

There was also something else on the streets you wouldn't have seen a few years ago. Hundreds of children, mostly Vietnamese, Cambodian, and Laotian, were using the mean streets as their playground. In front of drug addicts and winos they played hopscotch, stickball, tossed Frisbees, and tried to fly homemade kites in the narrow city canyons.

The Tenderloin was evolving. Slowly. We crossed Leavenworth near one of the toughest corners in the city. Emperor Norton Liquors was doing its usual brisk trade. But instead of its regulars wandering off to drink in alleys and hallways or in front of closed shops, they had gathered in front of the store to listen to a heavy-metal Laotion band playing double-triangle guitars in a mixture of hard rock and atonal Asian music on a makeshift stage in the street.

I slipped the T-Bird behind the stage and turned down Jones street, driving past the park that the Tenderloin Coalition had fought for six years to get. A patch of grass, a swing set, and a basketball court wasn't Tivoli Gardens but the people of the district had to start somewhere.

I pulled up in front of a store near the park, and Mickey and I got out of the car.

Painted across the store window in elaborately scrolled red and gold letters were the words DRAGON SEEDS. Under that, in simple block letters, were the words VIETNAM VETERANS ASSOCIATION. Taped to the window was a collection of signs. One read SUPPORT VVAWT—VIETNAM VETS AGAINST WAR TOYS. Not one of your more successful groups. Another read NICARAGUA IS SPANISH FOR VIET-NAM. And there were the practical signs. AA Meetings, Methadone Clinic Hours, shelter addresses, Agent Orange information, and AIDS warnings. The two largest signs in the window read FREE

BLEACH and FREE RUBBERS—WE HAVE EXTRA LARGE.

"Extra large?" Mickey asked.

"Beats me," I said.

An old set of Christmas bells jingled as I opened the door for Mickey. Inside there was more smoke that at an R. J. Reynolds board meeting.

The place had once been a lunch joint. There was a counter with cushionless stools. Old wooden tables and chairs filled the rest of the space. There was a rest-room sign that pointed to a door in the back that led to an alley. The walls were covered with movie posters: *Apocalypse Now, Platoon, The Deerhunter, Rambo I, Rambo II, The Green Berets.* The stuff would have jived up the Letterman lobby.

There were a half dozen men in the Dragon Seeds headquarters. Most of them were playing cards. A plastic chess set sat unused on an open board.

Four of the men were white and two were black. They all were wearing clothing that looked like it had been found in those Salvation Army deposit boxes you used to see in supermarket parking lots—until the stores decided to reclaim the parking spaces. Two of the white men had huge, bushy, colorless beards. Another one had a full orange beard that must have been dyed. The others were starting to grow beards as well or they just badly needed shaves. The two blacks wore San Francisco Giants baseball caps. They were all in their forties and they all looked sixty. Everyone was smoking something or other, from cigarettes to a cigar to a pipe. They had one other thing in common. They were all staring at Mickey.

"Can I be a service?" the black man closest to us said as he put down an AIDS comic book. Not a bad educational device for getting the information out to the people who needed it the most.

"We're looking for Curtis."

"Say why."

"Friends," I said. Which in fact was true. Mickey, the Chief, and I had met Curtis, Vietnam vet, recovering alcoholic, former black militant, former black Muslim, and current honcho of Dragon Seeds, during a kidnapping investigation. One of his vets, after years of hiding in the hills of Mendocino County, had been talked into coming out and moving to the city. A month later he kidnapped his own son from his ex-wife, who hired us when the police came up empty. Our investigation led us to Curtis who led us to the vet and the boy. We talked the woman into not pressing charges and split our fee with Dragon Seeds. The man ended up in a VA hospital and we wound up with a friend in the Tenderloin.

The man with the orange beard muttered an obscenity.

"Don't pay him no heed," one of the men with a colorless beard said. "That's Mr. Agent Orange. He don't trust shit. Excuse me, ma'am."

"No problem," Mickey said. "I'm used to Curtis."

Agent Orange just grunted.

"He back in the kitchen makin' lunch," the other black man said.

We moved through the tables. I pushed open the swinging door to the kitchen and saw Curtis standing over the stove, cooking something in a large pot. He stirred in some sliced carrots and put down the spoon.

Curtis was wearing a green shirt that advertised the Sizzler on Eddy and Leavenworth, blue jeans, and Nike Air hightops. His hair was cut short, revealing a receding hairline, which he compensated for with a neatly trimmed black goatee and mustache. His brown eyes, partially hidden behind horn-rimmed glasses, were alert and intelligent.

He was tall, six five or so, and lean and wiry. He was in good shape, which was something of a miracle. When he got back from a tour in Vietnam in '69, he was crazy,. He was run out of his hometown in rural Georgia and spent years drunk, homeless, and in a series of county jails. He finally ended up on Skid Row in L.A. It was religion that straightened Curtis out. First the Muslims, where he was Curtis X. and later born-again Christianity, where he abandoned the X. and all surnames forever. But that was a part of his life he seldom spoke about. And he didn't try to convert anyone through Dragon Seeds. It was enough if he could get them to use condoms and, if they were drug addicts, bleach.

Curtis was also wearing those hightops for a reason. When things were slow at headquarters, he played basketball at the new park across the street.

"How are things going?" I asked.

"Could be better. But what to expect when a third a the homeless out there are my vets?"

"It's tough," I said.

Curtis stared at me. He knew this wasn't a social call.

"We need some help," I said.

"An' I thought you come here to shoot some hoops with the
main man in our Tenderloin park."

"Ever see this guy?" I asked as I took out a copy of the composite photo.

"Look like a nice white boy. He play ball, too?"

"He could be a Vietnam vet," Mickey said.

"Don't look familiar, an' I see most of 'em."

"I know. That's why I came to you."

"Boy got a name?"

"Gutman. Vincent Gutman."

The sharp eyes cut into the picture. "This is a police composite
drawin', man. What's this dude wanted for?"

"Right now I see it as a missing person case."

He hesitated. "Could be anywhere. We got vets livin' in Golden
Gate Park. Hell, we had a Blood livin' in the damn bushes front a
the Federal Building. And that's only in the city. Don't know, man,
but I'll check aroun' an' keep my eyes open."

"He could be dangerous," Mickey said. "So don't let on if you
recognize him."

" 'Preciate the sound advice, ma'am," Curtis said as he picked
up a Da Nang baseball cap from a table and tipped it at her.
"Where this dude been since the war?" he continued.

"That's a hell of a good question. Could an MIA get out of Vietnam without the army knowing? I don't think he's been wandering
around here for sixteen years with amnesia."

"Only happen on soap operas," Curtis said. "On the other hand,
I heard some shit on the street. May be relevant."

"Like what?" I asked.

"Sounds. Jus' sounds."

"What kind?" I persisted.

" 'Bout some dude calls hisself a general."

"What about him?"

"I gotta investigate, man. You know how it is. See what I can do.

An' always 'preciate a visit from you and the lovely lady." He stirred whatever it was in the pot.

I decided I wouldn't get anywhere pressing him.

Mickey looked at me and said, "What about those April dates? Could they mean anything to Curtis—to Dragon Seeds?" Mickey was right. Maybe Curtis would have some line on the dates the April Fool Killer did his work.

"I don't date white women. 'Gainst my religion," Curtis said with a huge grin that revealed a perfect crescent of white teeth.

"In terms of Vietnam, we need to know whether certain dates have some particular meaning."

"Only date that got meanin' is the date you leave the damn jungle an' go back to the world."

"Try anyway. How about April 1?"

"April Fool? Hold on. This the April Fool Killer?"

"It's possible," Mickey said.

"Shee-it."

"What could April 1 have meant?" I persisted.

"To run the Dragon Seeds, you gotta be a historian for some a these guys. April 1 is the day last POW's released by Hanoi. In '73."

"Could be something," Mickey said.

" 'Specially if you were still a POW."

"Then we have April 11?"

"Don't ring no bells."

"How about April 17?" I asked.

"Oughta be on some TV quiz show. Khmer Rouge capture Phnom Penh."

"You're doing great. What about April 21?" I asked.

"Lotta men 'member that. Fall a Xuan Loc. Last defense 'fore Saigon. Vets remember twenty years ago better than yesterday."

"Anything big coming up this month? If this guy is using dates to mark events in Vietnam, what would be next?" Mickey asked.

Curtis stirred the contents of the pot. He picked up a large bone and put it in.

Mickey looked away.

Curtis thought it over. His face became lined. His light brown skin took on a grayish cast. He bit his lower lip.

"Got two a the biggest this month. April 29, 1975, the evacua-

tion of Saigon. April 30, 1975, the fall of Saigon. They mean somethin' if you still gave a shit about the war. For us it was over."

I thanked Curtis and gave him a donation for the Dragon Seeds.

"You can now deduct that contribution from your income taxes.
We a bona fide charity. All legal-like."

"Then give me a receipt."

"Sure thing." He reached into a drawer in one of the old kitchen
cabinets and pulled out a receipt book. He wrote me one. All legal-
like. Then he added, "You need help? A stakeout. A tail. Some
muscle. I got a lot a unemployed vets lookin' for work."

"Not a bad idea," Mickey said. "We'll definitely keep it in
mind."

"Yeah," I agreed.

"Now how 'bout some a my special stew?" he asked.

"So that's what you're cooking. We just had lunch," I lied.

"Come on, then, let's go shoot some baskets."

Curtis picked up the old Magic Johnson basketball that he kept
under the sink and bounced it on the floor.

"I'm not dressed for it," I complained.

"So you got an excuse when you lose at the black man's game."

"I've been thinking of taking up tennis again."

Mickey gave me a funny look. I smiled at her.

"He'd knock your jock off," she said.

"Course I will," Curtis said.

"She's talking about her tennis partner."

"Beat him, too," Curtis said as he dribbled the ball behind his
back.

We went back out into the smoke-filled room.

Curtis showed the picture around but no one recognized it.
Agent Orange wouldn't look at it.

As we went through the door Mickey pointed to the RUBBERS
sign and asked, "We have extra large?"

Curtis grinned. "Some a the home boys claim they too big to
wear one. So I tell 'em these are custom-made extra large. Make
'em proud to use 'em. Maybe keep the home boys and their ladies
alive."

We all laughed.

We crossed the street and went into the park. At one end of the basketball court six Vietnamese boys were playing half-court three-on-three ball.

Curtis suddenly stiffened and stopped. He was staring at the Vietnamese kids.

"What's wrong?" I asked.

"When I see 'em all together like that, it's like I'm back in Saigon." He took a deep breath. "I'm okay. I know that they ain't VC. But some vets can't take it. There been incidents. No dead Vietnamese yet. Not from a Dragon Seed. But some a the men are right on the edge."

We walked to the other end of the court. A chain net still hung from the rim. Pretty good anywhere. The people were taking care of their park.

I took off my jacket and undid my holster. No one seemed to notice the gun.

"You got hightops and I got shoes. I get the ball out."

"And she referees."

"Only if I don't have to move. I don't want to sprain an ankle in these heels."

"Okay with me. We go to eleven baskets," Curtis said.

I tried to keep it close with outside jump shots but I couldn't guard Curtis or rebound against him in my loafers.

I lost.

"I could have used a few calls, ref," I said.

"Better take up tennis, man," he said to me. "The white man's game."

"Give me that ball, wiseass," I said.

"New game to eleven," Curtis said as he tossed me the ball.

"Now watch his hands," I said to Mickey.

But Mickey wasn't paying attention to what I was saying.

She just looked at me, her eyes wide, and said, "Eleven. April 11 was the date on Gutman's tombstone."

Gutman's own special Vietnam date.

6

At the top of the Octavia Street hill sits Lafayette Park. On its north side, it overlooks the bay. Across Sacramento Street on its south side is a house once occupied by Sir Arthur Conan Doyle. The gateway to the green expanse of park is marked by two sable palms, each about thirty feet high. The park has jogging paths, a playground, rest rooms, benches, and, most importantly, two tennis courts.

I got up at dawn on Monday, the twenty-fifth of April, dressed in sweats and tennis shoes, got my old Arthur Ashe Head racket and some balls, and went outside. The morning air was cold and I could see my breath. I noticed that Nancy's car was gone. Walking north up Octavia was good stretching exercise for my stiff muscles. I passed the Christian school on one side of the street and the Buddhist temple on the other. Despite these competing presences, as far as I knew, there had never been a religious war on the street.

At a brisk pace it took me seven minutes to reach the park.

The courts were in a bowl at a lower level than the rest of Lafayette Park. I had to go down a dozen wooden steps sunk in the side of a hill to reach them. Surrounded by bushes and trees, the courts were shaded and chilly even when the sun was up.

That didn't stop me from getting in an hour of solo practice. I was rusty but very gradually the muscle memory began to return, thanks to years of high school and college tennis. Or so I thought. The winning is easy when there's no one on the other side of the net.

Back at the office, I showered, shaved, and dressed for the day. By nine-thirty I was still the only one there.

Shortly before ten Mickey and the Chief arrived.

"Not bad for a Monday morning," I said.

"We know," they said in unison. It was a game we played. None of us kept track of hours and Mickey and the Chief put in more than their share.

In my office, we all went over what Mickey and I had learned on Sunday at Letterman Hospital and at Dragon Seeds headquarters.

From the couch, Chief Moses said, "It is time to call the police."

"You're getting conservative, Chief," I said.

"I think he's right," Mickey retorted.

"Not yet," I insisted.

"If Curtis is right about the dates, and I'd bet he is, he's talking about the twenty-ninth and thirtieth, this Friday and Saturday."

"I know. I'll go to Homicide if there's another threat made by the April Fool Killer. I've told Nancy Gutman that already."

My partners reluctantly agreed that was fair enough.

"How are you going to find him?" The great tracker asked.

"First we find Gutman's former wife," I said.

"You will have to find her quickly," the Chief said.

"I'm one step ahead of you. Our client gave me her new married name and her birth date."

The Chief got up from the couch. "My help is not required here. I spoke to Tommy Dong. He is very unhappy about a new extortion attempt. I will look for Tran Van Dam." A few moments later he was gone on his hunt for the leader of the Yellow Suns. Van Dam had to be reminded of the deal we had cut. Reminding people was something the Chief was good at.

Mickey went back to her office and I got out the telephone book. I got the number of the California Department of Motor Vehicles and called. When I finally reached the right DMV clerk, I gave him the name, Barbara Gutman Shatts, and the essential element to get what I wanted, her date of birth. A few computer inputs later the clerk gave me all of the information printed on her driver's license—including her current address.

I invited Mickey along to see Barbara Shatts. The address I had for her was in Pittsburg, a city in the Delta about forty miles east of us. It had once been called Black Diamond, but after a steel mill went up inside the city limits, it changed its name to match the Pennsylvania steel giant—except for the "h" at the end of "burg."

From outside I heard the growling noise of a sanitation truck. All cars had to be off our street on Mondays from ten until noon for street sweeping. I checked my watch. It was already well past ten o'clock, which meant my car was in imminent danger of being towed away.

I told Mickey to lock up, jumped off the porch, and raced down the street. I had a fifty-yard lead on the tow truck that had appeared around the corner. The tow truck and I got to my T-Bird in a dead heat. While he lowered his chain I started the car and escaped.

Mickey was waiting for me on the porch.

"You ought to set your watch to go off Mondays at nine-thirty," she said as she got into the car.

"I keep forgetting to do it," I said.

"Here." She went through a sequence of button pushes on my digital Casio. "That'll take care of a month of Mondays."

With the next four Mondays taken care of, we drove off toward the Oakland Bay Bridge, an engineering feat at least as impressive as the Golden Gate to the west. The bridge itself is seven miles long and made up of three separate sections. The western part is a double suspension bridge anchored in the middle to a huge concrete pier. The eastern section is a cantilever bridge. Between the two parts is the Yerba Buena Island Tunnel. The bridges are double-decked to keep the traffic moving. Sell that myth to commuters at four in the afternoon. But this morning we cruised over at the speed limit.

We got off the bridge in Berkeley and made our way slowly through that university city to the tunnel through the Berkeley Hills and an open Highway 24. We passed Walnut Creek and Concord with their occasional BART subway stops. Rapid transit didn't do much out here to get people out of their cars. A BART subway isn't as much fun to ride as a cable car in the city.

We got to Pittsburg at noon.

"I'm hungry," Mickey announced.

"Making up for yesterday?"

"Don't remind me. I don't want to lose my appetite again."

I knew a fairly decent restaurant in the area, called the River-view, which operated on a barge docked in Antioch on the San Joaquin River. There in a booth overlooking the water we had a fine leisurely lunch of Pacific crabcakes and chilled asparagus.

The Railroad Avenue address in Pittsburg was easy enough to find. There was only one problem. The Shattses had moved and the current residents, who were standing in the doorway more or less talking to us, had no idea where.

They were a young couple, worse than young, a teenage couple. The boy had a bad case of acne and the girl was too skinny and needed a bath. He was wearing a brown Burger King uniform and she was dressed in a T-shirt that read "Pittsburg High" and jeans that looked like she had been poured into them. There was a baby crying in the background.

"How long have you lived here?" I asked the boy.

He shrugged.

"When did you move in?" Mickey tried.

The boy looked at his wife and then at me. She looked like she could use a dozen Whoppers right now. I showed them a ten spot.

"Yeah, that's more like it," the girl said.

The baby was howling.

"Damn that kid," she said as she turned and left.

The baby kept right on howling—louder.

I gave the boy the ten and he remembered that they had moved in two months ago. But he wasn't sure who had lived there before. The Shattses could have been ancient history. I let him close the door.

"Okay," I said to Mickey.

"If they just moved, she probably didn't get around to reporting the change to the DMV," Mickey said.

"If the Shattses were the prior tenants."

I asked at a Chevron full-service gas station where I could find the main post office. As I drove off with the directions Mickey noted, "You always say it isn't macho to ask for directions."

"Always?"

"Often."

Saved by the post office. I turned into the parking lot.

We went into a building that looked like a film director's idea of a Western jail.

I got in line behind a woman sending six boxes of shoes to Mexico. She spoke Spanish and the clerk only spoke English. The transaction was lengthy.

Finally at the window, I asked for a "Freedom of Information" form provided by Postal Service Regulation 262.73. If the Shattses had moved within eighteen months and left a forwarding address, the post office would provide it.

I went back to the writing area under the wanted posters to fill it out.

"Keep your eye out for women bearing packages," I told Mickey. I wasn't going to get caught like that again.

I filled out the form, got in line behind an empty-handed woman who only bought a book of stamps, paid the clerk the dollar fee, and got a new address for the Shatts family. I asked the clerk about it and she told me it was in a new housing development called Quail Point Homes between Pittsburg and Antioch.

"Now you know why I always send the Postmaster General a Christmas card every year," I said to Mickey as we went out to the lot.

We got back on the highway and came upon the Quail Point Homes sign almost immediately. We turned off and entered the development, drove past a row of models, and into a pattern of streets and cul-de-sacs with names that started with the letter A.

"Even you could find you way around here," Mickey said. Ignoring her, I drove over three blocks and found the Ds since the address we had was on Delta View.

Three minutes later we were parked in front of the Shattses' house. There was no view of the Delta but maybe that was asking too much from the developers.

We went up a paved walkway through a patch of ground that was beginning to show green shoots. There were a few small plants struggling under the front picture window. The house looked small, new, California expensive, and like every other third one on the street. It also looked a hell of a lot better than the apartment they had been living in. Parked in the driveway was a new blue Taurus.

"What's the routine?" Mickey asked.

"We're from the army lab," I said.

I rang the doorbell and heard musical chimes.

The door opened. The woman standing in front of us in a loose housecoat had fading reddish hair that was coming out of the bun she had pinned it in. She had a sharp nose and chin and small closely set gray-green eyes. There were lines around her eyes and mouth. She had been pretty once. Now she only looked like she hadn't slept for a week.

A bony little girl of about five with large saucer eyes was hanging on to her skirt.

"Mrs. Barbara Gutman Shatts?" I asked.

"Yes?"

I took out the card I had picked up at Koyota's office. With a little deft work I had been able to change the name. "We're with the Army Identification Lab. We'd like to talk to you about Vincent Gutman." I quickly pocketed the card.

Her face turned somewhere between light gray and ash white.

"Can we come in?" Mickey asked.

"Of course. I'm sorry."

She led us into a sparsely furnished living room. The only things that looked finished in it were a fireplace and a wood and glass gun cabinet next to it that was full of all kinds of weapons from shotguns to pistols. I admired the collection.

"One of my husband's hobbies," she said. "Sit down. Please. We're a little short on furniture. The new stuff was supposed to be delivered last week, but you know how it is."

We sat on the two upholstered chairs in the room. Mrs. Shatts brought in a wood chair from the kitchen for herself. She sent the little girl, whose name was Jessica, into another room to play.

"Cute kid," I said.

"Thank you. Can I get you anything?"

"We just need some information," Mickey said.

"There is some question about the identification of your late husband's remains," I said.

"What?"

I looked at Mickey. "The dental records didn't check out," I said.

"His dental records? I don't understand. Why are you doing this now?" she asked.

"The army is reviewing some of its early identifications. We're a lot more technically sophisticated than we were in '72."

She collapsed back into her chair. "What are you trying to tell me?" she asked.

"That Vincent Gutman may be alive," Mickey said.

"That's impossible."

"Not impossible. And if he's alive, he may try to contact you," she said.

"How could he find me?"

"We did," I said.

She sat up stiffly. "I don't belive he's alive."

I was explaining again how Gutman's remains could have been misidentified when her current husband opened the front door.

We stood up and Barbara introduced us to Clyde. Clyde was about five ten and muscular, with a wisp of a mustache. He had thinning brown hair and wore a tan corduroy jacket with a brown and yellow plaid shirt open at the neck. We shook hands. He had a strong grip. Based on the books he was carrying, I made him for a teacher at the local community college. I asked him.

"No," Barbara said, answering for him, "Clyde teaches at the high school. He could have gone to the college when it opened up but he decided not to."

"I prefer teaching younger students," he explained. "You have a chance to mold them."

Mickey and I both nodded.

"I'll get you a chair," Barbara said to him. She brought out another kitchen chair.

"They're here about Vincent," Barbara blurted out.

"Vincent?"

"Vincent Gutman." I said the name very slowly.

"The man's been dead for sixteen years," Clyde said.

I repeated the misidentification story for Clyde's benefit.

"I tell you the man is dead," Clyde insisted.

"He may not be. If he's not, he may try to contact his wife," Mickey said.

"I don't believe this!" Clyde shouted.

"If he does, would you give this agency a call." I gave him one of our St. John Agency cards. "It's a front for one of our army under-cover operations," I explained.

"Isn't this compromising security?" Clyde asked.

"We know you're loyal Americans. You're not the kind of people we worry about."

Clyde shrugged and took the card. I gave Barbara her own just in case.

"We met your daughter," Mickey said. "Charming little girl."

"Thank you," Clyde said.

"Is Jackie around?" I asked Barbara.

"Jackie?" Clyde answered. "What's she got to do with all this?"

This was information I wanted for Nancy Gutman but it certainly wasn't irrelevant. "Gutman may want to see his daughter," I said.

"Good luck," Clyde said.

"What do you mean?" I asked.

There was an uncomfortable silence. Barbara was fidgeting in her chair.

"The kid ran away when she was in high school," Clyde explained.

"That had to be a while ago."

"Four years," Barbara said.

"She was impossible," Clyde said.

His wife's small eyes grew even smaller as they teared up. "We hired a detective and he traced her to the Silver Bar Casino in North Tahoe," Barbara said. "She was working as a blackjack dealer."

"We went to Nevada to try to bring her home," Clyde said. "But she went crazy. Screamed obscenities at us. Told us she never wanted to see us again. I figured she was on drugs. What a waste of time. And money."

"I don't know what we even did to her," Barbara said.

"We didn't do anything to her. She just turned out bad. I see it happen in school all the time," Clyde said angrily.

"How long ago did you see her in Nevada?" I asked.

"Three years."

"Is she still there?" I asked.

"Who the hell knows," Clyde said.

I looked at Barbara. She lowered her eyes. "Her grandmother would like to know where she is," I said.

"I lost touch with Nancy. One of those things that just happens."

I gave her Nancy's address

"Do you have a picture of Jackie?"

"Of course," Barbara said.

Clyde just grunted. He took out a cigarette and lit it as his wife went to get a photo album.

"Can't smoke at the damn school. Or most other places these days," Clyde said as he took a deep drag. "At least a man's home is his castle." The castle filled with a gray cloud of smoke.

Barbara came back in, showed us a picture, and said, "This is the latest one we have. It's a high school photo."

The girl was beautiful. Reddish hair like the mother once had but more of a resemblance to her grandmother except the large eyes were green.

"Could we borrow this?" I asked.

"Oh, God, keep it," Barbara said. Then she whispered, "I have more prints."

"Thanks," I said.

"Do you think Vincent will find her?" Barbara asked

"He's dead!" Clyde insisted.

"If he's alive, he'll want to find her," I said.

"And you're the obvious way," Mickey added.

"Oh, God!" Barbara began to cry.

Clyde stood up, making it clear that the interview was over. The man wanted his castle to himself.

I thanked them for their help and reminded them to call the agency, not the army, if Gutman contacted them. I didn't mention anything about the April Fool Killer but some kind of warning was in order.

"I hope you can use those guns," I said.

"Damn right I can."

"Gutman may be dangerous," I said.

"I can take care of my family." Clyde unlocked the gun case and took out a Colt .45. He opened the cylinder and showed me that he kept it loaded.

"You'll do fine," Mickey said.

We left the house. A Datsun the color of mud was parked next to the Taurus. The car was old enough to have been produced before the Japanese started hiring French painters as consultants for their automobile colors.

We discussed the couple as we drove into the city against the gridlock starting to form in the eastbound lanes.

"Something terribly wrong there..." Mickey began.

"Woman's gut intuition?"

"Yeah. Why not?"

"Was anyone lying?" I asked. Mickey is good at detecting those little nuances of gesture and body language that suggest a person is lying.

We entered the Berkeley tunnel, where traffic was beginning to back up. A curtain of darkness fell.

When we came back into the light, Mickey said, "I'm not sure."

"Barbara was hiding something," I said.

"What?"

"I don't know. But she was a lot more uncomfortable after Clyde arrived."

"And real uncomfortable talking about Jackie."

"This will take some following up," I concluded.

Mickey agreed.

We stopped behind a line of cars at a red light in Berkeley. I had plenty of time to notice that we were across the street from Reggie Jackson Chevrolet—which is what happens to old ball players. If they're smart, they get richer. It took us three changes to get through the intersection. Almost enough time to go in and buy a car. I was surprised Mickey didn't suggest it.

"What about their move from that cheap apartment to the middle-class suburbs?" Mickey said. "And a new car in front."

"Obviously they came into some money. The question is how."

"But Clyde still drives an old brown Datsun."

"Probably not for much longer," I said as I went through the toll booth and entered the eastern cantilevered section of the Bay Bridge. One more tunnel to go., The traffic stopped dead in front of me. It was parking lot time for the commute.

At the office, we went over our day with the Chief.

He mulled over our story and concluded: "The woman would

not have abandoned the daughter so easily." Then he told us about his meeting with Tran Van Dam. The Vietnamese gang leader, fearing for his gonads, denied breaking the agreement.

"He convinced me, for now, that it was not the Yellow Suns back in the extortion business."

"Where do we go from here?" I asked.

"Tommy has refused to pay any protection money, so his operation is threatened. Tran has agreed to use his gang members to stake out some of Tommy's poker houses. They do not like outsiders extorting money from other Vietnamese."

"A paradox," I said.

"No. If they do it, it is all right. The money stays in the Vietnamese community," the Chief explained.

"Slightly redistributed," Mickey said.

"Van Dam says he is like 'Robin the Hood,'" the Chief continued and laughed. "He also promised to catch these men and cut off their schlongs. His English is improving."

"So we have our own Vietnamese army at work," I said.

"And well motivated," Chief Moses added.

"But where do we go on the Gutman case?" Mickey asked.

"If he makes a threat, we have to go to the police. If he doesn't, it'll be a bitch finding him. All I can see us doing is concentrating on the people he might contact. Barbara and his daughter."

"What about the mother herself?" the Chief asked.

"She would have told me."

"Not necessarily," Chief Moses said.

I called Nancy and she denied any contact with Vincent. She was annoyed with my question but softened when she realized I was just doing the job she was paying me to do. I hung up the phone and got up and looked out of the front office window. I turned to Mickey, who was working on her Mac. "It should be light out for a while yet. How about if we hit some tennis balls in the park?"

"I know what you're doing, Jeremiah," Mickey said.

"How about you, Chief?"

He grunted. "Too many brats play tennis. I am going to make use of your upstairs basketball court. How about joining me for that?"

"No. I have a mission."

"An impossible one," Mickey said. "But okay. I'll hit some with you. I could use the exercise."

"I'll get the rackets."

"You really think you're going to beat Glenn?"

"Women like men to fight over them," I said.

"But not with just tennis rackets for weapons, " Chief Moses added.

"I'll beat you myself," Mickey said, ignoring our comments.

"Thank you, Martina."

Chief Moses applauded.

I went upstairs to get the gear. When I came back down, I handed her an old wooden Davis racket.

"Geez. What's this? You lift this from a museum? Next time I'll bring my own." She took several forehand swings.

The Chief, who she almost hit with one of her swings, took the stairs two at a time for basketball and safety. I resisted the old urge to go one-on-one with him and forget tennis.

I hoped Mickey didn't realize tennis with me meant missing her Dr. Earnhard's nightly spot on the tube. Maybe when she did, if she asked nicely, I would talk about tennis elbow and rotator cuff injuries to make up for it.

7

Even with the old racket, Mickey taught me how far I had let my game slip.

Tuesday morning at dawn I was on the courts again—alone. My back and shoulders were stiff and tight in the cold but I got myself warm enough to loosen the muscles. My serve needed the most work and I tried to recall the fundamentals. Loosen your Continental grip on the handle; toss the ball out high and to your right; scratch your back with the edge of the racket; and brush the ball with the strings left to right for spin. I remembered the routine about a third of the time and executed it about twenty-five percent of the time. But it was coming back. I could feel it. And I was motivated.

When my right shoulder began to ache, I called it quits. I gathered up my gear, left the park, and walked back down Octavia. My neighbors were coming out of the rows of Victorians, heading off to work on another beautiful day.

I picked up the April 26 edition of *The Chronicle* lying on my porch. As I disarmed our digital computer alarm I scanned the front page. At the bottom was a small headline: AFK THREATENS AGAIN. The story was about the latest death threat from the April Fool Killer. He promised deaths on April 29 and April 30, just as Curtis had predicted.

Despite the early hour, I called Curtis, who usually slept at the Dragon Seeds headquarters. He complained about being awakened but he didn't hang up.

"Any word about Gutman on the street?" I asked.

"Nothin', man."

"What about this general you were talking about?"

"Gimme some time."

"You were right about the dates," I said. "The April Fool Killer sent another death threat."

"Got somethin' right," he said.

"Keep trying to get a line on the both of them. But be careful."

"That's my middle name," Curtis said and hung up.

When my partners arrived, I brought them back into my office and showed them the newspaper headline.

"We've seen it," Mickey said.

"Now you must go to the police," Chief Moses said.

Mickey agreed.

Someone stepped on the front porch and the red warning light went on at my desk. A female messenger appeared on the video scanner.

"I'll get it," Mickey volunteered. She got up and went into the reception area. A minute later she came back with a brown manila envelope.

"From the jury-research firm." She handed me the envelope.

I opened it and found a memo and a list of the names of jurors in a certain jury pool. I read the memo, then looked up. "It's a rush job. A major drug-trafficking case." I handed the list of names to the Great Tracker.

"The usual information?" he asked.

"Right. Including photographs."

"And you will go to the police?" he asked.

"Mickey and I are on our way."

We put on the answering machine and locked up the office. The Chief went off to look for his King Cab pickup truck and Mickey and I collected the T-Bird, which was only three blocks away.

We drove to the precinct house and got lucky. A few of the visitor parking spaces were not taken up by illegally parked police cars and I quickly pulled into one.

We went through the double main doors and through a metal

detector. Mickey and I had been smart enough to leave our pieces at home. No sense in setting off alarms. Of course, if we had been carrying plastic handguns or plastic explosives, the detector would be worthless anyway. Maybe someday detector technology would catch up to terrorist technology.

We went into the muster room on the main floor, where a sergeant sat at a desk high as a judge's bench. An American flag stood to his right, a flag of California to his left. A picture of the new mayor had replaced that of his predecessor, Dianne Feinstein. I missed the old picture. Ex-beauty queen Mayor Dianne was a hell of a lot cuter.

I knew the building well. Vice was down in hell, next to Narcotics and the locker rooms, showers, toilets, and holding cells. On the second floor were Homicide, Robbery, and Burglary, along with interrogation rooms, the clerks and administration.

The desk sergeant, a heavyset gray-haired cop in his fifties, hardly looked at our IDs. He spent most of the time checking out Mickey, who in a knee-length skirt and red sweater looked eminently checkable. He signed us in and gave us visitor badges.

We walked past a bulletin board of wanted posters. I looked for my favorite, a classic WANTED—DEAD OR ALIVE—BILLY THE KID poster, but some humorless cop or administrator had taken it down. We went up a flight of metal steps that rang under Mickey's heels and turned right on the landing into Homicide. The large windows that ran all around the room had been washed since I had last been there. The clean light pouring in was a definite improvement.

I was looking for Detective Johnny Dajewski, a Polish cop with rawboned good looks and tousled crayon-yellow hair. Everybody called him Johnny D., including his Mexican wife, who, according to Johnny, was finally learning some English after six years of marriage. I figured their marriage would soon be in trouble.

Johnny D. was at a desk in the middle of the division bullpen. He was typing a report on an ancient machine by the classic hunt-and-peck method. He looked up and smiled at Mickey.

He had on a blue shirt that was frayed at the collar and sleeves and a bluish tie that looked like it had been dunked along with a doughnut in his morning coffee. His wrinkled green suitcoat hung over the back of his chair. He was wearing a shoulder holster and gun which made up some for the rest of the look.

"What's up?" he asked.

"You mean you're glad to see us?" I asked.

"I'm always glad to see your pretty partner."

As cop and P.I., we were friendly adversaries. Johnny, in fact, owed me for several favors. As I saw it I was about to do him another one.

Mickey sat on the edge of his desk and I pulled up a chair.

"I've got some information about the April Fool Killer," I offered.

Johnny whistled.

I went through Nancy's story for him.

"This guy Gutman's officially dead?"

"That's what the records show."

"But you don't believe it."

"He could be alive. My client made a convincing case for it."

"Where's he been since 1972?" Johnny asked.

"Amnesia. Or in Vietnam. An MIA who was found," I said.

"Then the government's gotta know about him."

"They don't seem to," Mickey said.

Johnny was shaking his head as Detective Oscar Chang, another favorite adversary of mine, came into the bullpen. I hoped he would continue on to his private glass-enclosed office, but no such luck. He came right for us, looking like someone about to go for the jugular. Mine.

"What are you doing here, St. John?" he asked with no trace of politeness. He glanced at Mickey but focused on me. Some men you can't distract.

Oscar Chang was the opposite of his partner, Johnny D. He was dressed in a neatly pressed dark suit with a starched white shirt and dark silk tie. His black hair was precisely parted and stiff with tonic. They could have posed for a before-and-after fashion ad for *GQ*.

When Chang was angry or upset, his coal-black irises bulged, giving him a fish-eyed look.

In an earlier case, Chang had been on the wrong side of the law and I had covered for him with the D.A. Seeing me reminded him that he also owed me one, which he resented.

"I have some information you might find useful," I said.

"You are like a bad penny. You keep turning up."

"You can do better than that," Mickey said.

"Some of my proverbs are not suitable when a lady is present."
Mickey smiled. It was beautiful. Even Chang loosened up.

"I came here to do you a favor," I said.

"What kind?" Chang asked.

"I told you. Information. It's a possible lead in the April Fool
Killer case."

Chang closed his eyes. He meditated a minute and motioned us
to follow him. "Come with me. All of you."

We moved our conversation to the privacy of Chang's office. It
was crowded but we each had a seat. Chang shut the glass door
and sat down behind his metal desk.

"What do you have?"

Mickey and I repeated what we had told Johnny, from Nancy's
arrival at my office to the visit to Koyota.

Chang sighed. "So you believe this Gutman is alive?"

"Chances are good."

"What's your part in this now?" Chang asked.

"Missing person. Gutman's daughter. Last heard of at the Silver
Bar Casino at Tahoe. Anything comes up about her, I'd appreciate
the help."

"Technically, you should have come to us sooner," Chang said.

"With a dead man as a suspect?"

Chang smiled for a change. "I will overlook it. But now I want
you out of it. You are not to look for Gutman. Is that clear? Do not
get in my way."

"We're looking for the daughter," Mickey chimed in earnestly.

"As of right now so are we. If you find her, let us know. And if
your client is withholding evidence, I assume you will give her the
correct legal advice."

"I passed the state bar exam," I said.

"Act like it," Chang said as he got up. The interview was over.

In the car we agreed our next move was a conversation with the
April Fool Killer's sole survivor, Jacob Stein.

We got a parking space in front of the office. I took it as a good
omen. No messages on the answering machine. As we turned it off
Johnny D. called. I signaled to Mickey to pick up the phone at her
desk.

"I appreciated what you gave us, Jeremiah, no matter what Chang said."

"I'd just like a little reciprocation."

He was almost whispering. "I can't give you stuff on the murders directly but this could help you with the daughter. If that's your real goddamned case. There may be a Nevada connection. Two of the victims took a casino tour to Reno and two of the others visited Nevada in the past two months."

"Some connection. Everybody goes to Nevada."

"Shit. I gotta hang up." Johnny was gone.

Mickey hung up the other line. "Does that change our plans?"

"Not at all. We ask Stein about Nevada."

"But first let's eat lunch," she said.

"I've got some cold cuts upstairs."

"Okay. It'll be quick."

We sat at my Formica Kitchen table eating sandwiches of pickled peppers, Sonoma Jack cheese, and roast beef. In deference to her diet, Mickey drank water and refused the jalapeno-flavored chips. I went for the chips and a Henry's.

I looked up Stein's law office in the phone book. He was on Montgomery Street.

"Should we make an appointment?" I asked.

"Let's surprise him," Mickey said.

I called to see if he was in. I didn't want the surprise to be on us. When I found that he was, I hung up.

We walked over to California Street to get a cable car. I put two dollars into the sleek new ticket-dispensing machine, and we waited for one of the red and gold cars to arrive. Ten minutes later we were on our way downtown.

Stein's office was in an old gray stone building. The lobby was small and there was only one elevator. He was on the second floor. The elevator clanged down and rattled open to reveal an old-fashioned cage and a closed metal gate. Mickey and I decided jointly on the steps.

JACOB STEIN ATTORNEY-AT-LAW was stenciled in black on a glass door located in a very narrow hallway. This was a one-man operation. There was a pretty blond woman in a tan business suit and beige ruffled blouse at the receptionist desk in the empty waiting room.

So far I had not seen any sign of police protection for Stein, unless a cop was hiding in a closet.

I gave the woman our agency card. She stood up. She was well over six feet tall. And she moved quickly. The woman was in and out of Stein's private office before we could open a magazine.

"Please go in."

Jacob Stein was sitting behind an old wooden desk in front of a single high window that looked out on the street below. There were law degrees and certificates on the wall but no pictures. Your basic bare-bones operation that I understood well.

"Sit down," Jacob Stein said.

We did. Jacob Stein was the most unlikely Jewish lawyer I'd ever seen. The wavy black hair, the thick mustache, the broad nose, the liquid brown eyes, and the brown skin would have led me to assume Chicano.

"I know what you're thinking. How does a Jewish lawyer get to look like a Mexican-American?" He grinned with perfect white teeth and jabbed his finger into the air.

"Something like that."

"I changed my name in law school. It's all legal. See. Jacob Stein on all the diplomas." He pointed to the collection of framed papers on the wall.

"Why?" I asked, even though I thought I knew the answer.

"Yes. Why?" Mickey echoed.

He looked at both of us and threw up his arms. "Even Chicanos want a Jewish lawyer. Not one named Geraldo Garcia. But one who can speak Spanish." He poked at himself with his forefinger.

"Does it work?" I asked.

"Yes. As you can see I have a low overhead. It keeps rates down. A lot of my clients are poor. Illegal aliens. Some seeking amnesty. Latin American refugees seeking political asylum. Migrant workers with big families, trying to survive on the minimum wage. They need their rights protected too." He picked up our business card. "But I take it you are not here to discuss my practice."

"No," I said, "We want to ask you some questions about the April Fool Killer."

"I told the police everything I know. Why should I talk to a couple of private dicks?"

"Private dicks?" Mickey said and groaned.

Stein looked sheepish.

"It's important to our client," I said.

"Who is?" he asked, recovering from his momentary embarrassment.

"Client confidentiality."

"I'm not impressed. Why should I talk to you?"

"If we run into any Chicanos who need a lawyer, we know where to direct them," I said.

Stein sighed. He looked skeptical but said, "All right. All right. Go ahead. Ask."

"Any reason you can think of for the attack? Why you were picked to be a victim?"

"No."

"Anything in your past that might be relevant?" Mickey asked.

"Now just hold it a minute. I told the police and I will tell you. I can't figure it. I don't have a clue. I know it is hard to believe but maybe it was random."

"Maybe," I said. It was hard to believe.

"What exactly happened the night of the attack?" Mickey asked.

"I was closing my office late on a Thursday night. I was alone in the hall. Suddenly this guy comes out of the men's room and starts walking behind me. He seems in a hurry and I stop to let him go by. The next thing I know he has me in a choke hold with a knife at my ribs."

"What did you do?" I asked.

"I offered him my wallet."

"What did he say?" I asked.

"'I want your life, fucker.' So I yelled out, 'Who the hell are you?' and he says, 'April Fool,' and raises the knife to stab me. I knew about the three other murders. I knew I was in the hands of a psychopath. I unleashed karate on him. Caught him by surprise. He tried to fight me when I broke his hold, but he was losing. So he bolted down the stairs. I went after him but he was too fast. I went back to my office and called the police."

"Then what?" Mickey asked.

"I went to a bar and got drunk on tequila. I can change my name but not my tastes."

"You gave the police a good description," Mickey said.

58   WILLIAM BABULA

"You don't forget the face of a man who was trying to kill you."

"Were you in the Vietnam War?" Mickey asked.

"No. Actually I was a conscientious objector."

"Do you know a man named Vincent Gutman?" she asked.

"No. Should I?"

"That depends," she said.

Jacob Garcia Stein leaned forward. "You know . . ." he began, his tone impatient. This Q&A was beginning to annoy him.

"Why no police protection?" Mickey asked, shifting gears.

"My clients don't want a cop hanging around. You can under-stand that. Besides, I can take care of myself."

"You demonstrated that," I said.

He unwrapped a large cigar and lit up without asking if we minded. Mickey started to wave at the smoke. Stein turned on one of those smoke-eating machines on his desk. It helped some.

"Anything else?" he asked, waving and jabbing with the cigar.

"One other thing. We're looking for someone. A missing per-son," Mickey said.

"This Vincent Gutman?" he asked.

"Possibly."

"I said I never heard of him. Who is he?"

"You were in Nevada in the past two months?" I asked, ignoring his question.

"Yes. In Reno," he punctuated his statement with a cigar jab.

"Do you remember seeing this woman?" I took out the picture of Jackie Gutman.

He put down the cigar and took the picture and studied it. "I would remember this woman if I had seen her."

"Maybe you just saw her briefly," Mickey said.

"No. Where would I have seen her?"

"Possibly at the tables. She has been a dealer."

"Sorry." He passed the picture back to me abruptly and picked up his cigar. He held it still in front of his face. "Is she your missing person?"

"Yes. If anything comes to mind, would you give me a call?" I asked.

"Who is looking for her?" he asked.

"My client," I said. "And maybe a few other people."

"Sure. If I think of anything. But what's her connection to the April Fool Killer?"

"She may be his daughter," Mickey said.

Jacob Stein went pale.

We left before he could ask more questions. We used the stairs again. Inside the elevator someone started ringing the emergency bell.

"Wise decision, the stairs," I said.

Out on the street the high rises of Montgomery were blocking the sun and a cold wind was blowing through the gray canyon formed by the buildings. We walked toward California Street and the cable car.

"I didn't believe him," Mickey said.

"Why not?"

"The way he froze when he saw the photo of Jackie Gutman. All of his cigar jabbing stopped. The man had been reached."

"I can buy that," I agreed. "He seemed to be telling the truth about Gutman but he sure looked and sounded different when he saw Jackie's picture."

We climbed on the cable car.

"What's next?" Mickey asked over the sound of clanging bells.

"I know it's a long shot but there might be something to the Nevada connection," I said.

"So?" Mickey asked.

"So we talk to Barbara Shatts again tomorrow. Get her to close some gaps. Then on to Nevada."

Back at the office I made several calls, including one to Nancy explaining that I had gone to the police with the information she gave me.

"I know," she said. "They've been here."

"What did you tell them?"

"Just that the picture in the newspaper resembled my son. They wanted to know if he had contacted me. He hasn't."

We now had two teams at work. There wasn't going to be much need for mine.

"Why don't you just leave it to the police now?" I suggested.

"No, Jeremiah." She hung up.

At five o'clock I offered to take Mickey to the Hyde Street Grille

if she would come out on the court with me again. The wind had
died down and it had warmed up.

"The Hyde Street Grille again? Don't you know that San Francisco has over 4,200 eating places?"

I made some quick calculations. "That comes to ninety per
square mile."

"So in the square mile around us you keep picking the same
place."

"Okay. We'll try someplace else."

"It's after five and I'm going home. I don't want to play tennis.
I'm going to get out a frozen Weight Watchers Dinner and watch
Glenn's spot on TV... besides, I've got to pack." She shut down her
Mac. Before I could argue with her, she was gone.

A half hour later the Chief called in to report that his work with
the jury pool was going well.

I went out to look for a new restaurant. The wind had picked up
again and the evening promised to be cold. I wandered along Van
Ness and, instead of finding one of those other eighty-nine restaurants to eat in, I located a new tennis pro shop. I took two demo
rackets home to try out.

8

Wednesday was either another perfect day or another diurnal rotation toward drought, depending upon your point of view. It was also two days away from the next threatened murder. Leaving the rain dances to Chief Moses, I accepted the weather and went up to the courts early in the morning to try out the two demo rackets. There was a short baldheaded guy in his sixties looking for someone to hit with and I obliged. He introduced himself as Cy as we went out on the court.

Cy used so much topspin and backspin that the tennis ball acted like a Ping-Pong ball in a typhoon. But at least under those adverse conditions I was able to decide which racket I preferred.

Back at the apartment I showered, shaved, dressed, and packed a suitcase for Nevada. I made room reservations at a place I knew in Incline. With everything set, I went downstairs to my office.

At nine o'clock, I heard the Chief come in. He didn't look happy.

"Tommy Dong called me last night. There has been an arson attempt at one of his poker parlors."

"I thought the Rising Suns had them staked out."

The Chief flopped down on the couch. "Not all of them. This one was up in Sonoma. And get the name straight. These are the Yellow Suns."

Sonoma was a fairly quiet town some thirty-five miles northeast of the city in Jack London's Valley of the Moon. It was known for its historic town plaza, for the Bear Flag monument recognizing it as the site of the short-lived California Republic, for the last Spanish mission in the chain of twenty-one that reached north from San Diego in the 1820's, for Buena Vista, the oldest premium winery in the state, for General Vallejo's home, for the restored 1985 Toscano Hotel, for a cheese factory, and for tourists. Lots of tourists. And a low crime rate. A poker parlor was about as far as Sonoma went for public vice. Unfortunately, the crime rate had just taken a quantum leap.

"What do you think?"

"It makes me suspicious once again of Tran Van Dam."

"Any damage?" I asked.

"Minor. But Tommy received a call after the attempt. Pay up or there will be a real fire."

"I assume he's not going to pay," I said.

"Correct. Instead we are going to set a trap." Chief Moses got up. He looked out of the window at the backyard. "Your land is dying."

I had heard this before. "We're supposed to conserve water," I said.

He just shook his mane of black hair in disgust. "First you waste what the Great Spirit gives. Then you let the earth dry up and call it conservation."

Chief Moses never mentioned the Great Spirit unless he was genuinely moved, greatly pissed, or just joking around.

"What's your next move?" I asked.

"Van Dam will now cover them all with his gang."

"I thought you didn't trust him."

"I will give him one more chance." He pushed himself up from the couch. That was one of the Chief's shortest stays on it.

As he started for the front door I called, "What about the juror profiles?"

"Do not worry." The door opened. "There is time." The door closed. The Chief was gone.

I carried my suitcase and the two demo rackets out to the car—which was right in front of the building—and opened the trunk. I saw Mickey coming around the corner at Austin Street. She was wearing a light coat and moving with athletic grace, despite the heels she wore and the suitcase she carried. I could never convince her to wear running shoes to get here and then to change at the office. She thought running shoes made her legs look short and stubby. Impossible. But you can't argue with a woman's self-perception—not even a *Playboy* model's.

I put her suitcase in the trunk and we went inside. Under her coat, Mickey had on a buttery yellow cable sweater and gray skirt. The skirt was just long enough to pass for businesslike but the V-neck of the sweater was cut just a bit low for most businesses.

"What time do we leave?" she asked as she sat down on the couch.

"Soon as we can. This time we'll be there early. While Clyde's at the high school."

"So let's go," she said as she got up and smoothed her skirt.

We turned on the answering machine, shut off the video scanner, and armed the digital alarm. The first-floor office was safe behind bars.

I drove to Van Ness and parked by a meter a few stores away from the tennis shop.

"Why are we stopping?" she asked.

"I've got to see a man about a racket."

I got the demo rackets out of the trunk and carried them into the pro shop. I went with the wide-bodied racket and tipped the stringer ten bucks to do it while I waited. He did the job on an Alpha machine with amazing speed—stringing the racket at fifty-five pounds tension with synthetic gut. It all cost me $230 plus tax and the ten-buck bribe.

I rushed out to the car, deposited the new racket in the trunk, and got in behind the wheel.

"You're nuts. A new racket's not going to help you."

"We'll see." I pulled out into the heavy flow of Van Ness traffic and headed for the Oakland Bay Bridge. Mickey put on KRQR—the Rocker FM station. I usually listened to KSFO—Home of the A's and Rock-'n'-Roll Classics—unless I had the Chief along. He favored KFDC from Palo Alto—FM Concert Hall. This was why we seldom played the radio in the office.

Bridge traffic and the traffic through Berkeley were light. The morning commute was ending. Somewhere near Concord we lost the station and I shut the radio off. We passed the BART subway station, end of the line to the East Bay, and the Concord Park-and-Ride lot—the one with the worst record of car thefts in the Bay Area.

At Delta View the blue Taurus was still parked in the driveway. Barbara Shatts, as we expected, answered the door. Her daughter Jessie had her arms wrapped around her mother's knees.

"You're back?"

"Sorry. But we have a few things we need to check," I explained.

"The furniture still hasn't arrived," Barbara said as she led us into the living room. She was dressed in slacks, a sweater, and a jacket. Her red hair hung loose down to her shoulders. Her small features looked less pinched than I remembered. "We were just going out shopping," she added.

"This shouldn't take long," I said as Mickey and I took the same two upholstered chairs as on our last visit. Barbara sent Jessie to her room and brought out a kitchen chair.

"What can I do for you this time?" Barbara asked.

"You can tell us what you left out last time," I said.

Barbara bit her lip. "I don't know what you're talking about."

"There's a Nevada connection. Gutman contacted you, didn't he? He wanted to see his daughter and you sent him to Nevada."

"No. No. That's not true." Barbara's tiny gray-green eyes teared up. Her sharp chin quivered.

"Come on," Mickey said.

"No. No." She covered her eyes with her hands.

"We just want to protect you and your daughter. Gutman is a very dangerous man. But we need the truth from you."

"What do you mean?"

"He may be the April Fool Killer," I said.

"I know. I've seen the newspapers," Barbara said as she looked up. She brushed the tears from her cheek. She got up and came back with a handful of pink tissues.

"Okay," she said softly.

"Vincent called, didn't he?" I asked.

She nodded her head and said, "Yes."

"What did he want?"

"To find Jackie."

"What about you?" Mickey asked.

"I told him about Clyde and Jessica. He understood. He said he was out of my life."

Pretty reasonable for a psychopath, I thought. "When did he call?" I asked.

"I don't remember exactly. Sometime in March."

"March," I repeated and looked at Mickey. It made sense.

"Why didn't you tell us this before?" Mickey asked.

Barbara started to cry in earnest. We waited through three tissues.

"Clyde said not to tell anyone."

"So you told Clyde about the call?" I asked.

"Of course."

"Of course," Mickey repeated.

"Why didn't Clyde want you to tell anyone?" I asked.

Barbara was shaking her head. Her face was flushed and a pattern of freckles was visible across her nose and cheeks.

"I'm not sure. He was just very upset. He said we shouldn't get involved. And he was angry that I had told Vincent anything about Jackie."

"She's his daughter," I said.

"I don't know. He was just angry."

"What exactly did you tell Vincent?" Mickey asked.

She folded her hands. "I gave him the name of the Silver Bar Casino. That's all. I mean she's not even there anymore."

That suggested she knew more than she was telling. "Where is she now?" I asked.

"I don't know!" she insisted.

I pulled back. "Jackie's birth date?"

She collected herself and gave it to us.

"Any close friends at the casino?" Mickey asked.

"At first she mentioned a roommate. A Sherry Wine."

"A dealer?" I asked.

"No. She was a showgirl."

"Anyone else? She must have had a friend among the dealers."

Barbara thought it over. "She mentioned an Opal...Chesko, I think her name was. She dealt blackjack, too."

"Anybody else?" I asked.

She sat up stiffly in the chair. "No."

"Did you give Vincent these names?" Mickey asked.

"Yes," she whispered.

"Did Vincent tell you where he had been all these years?" I asked.

"He actually said he'd been dead. I didn't understand him."

"Have you heard from him since?" I asked.

"No. I told you. He promised to leave us alone."

"Then you don't know if he located Jackie?" Mickey asked.

The pitch of her voice rose as she said, "No. Of course not."

"I don't believe you," I said.

Barbara started to cry again. We waited. "Please don't say anything to Clyde. Jackie's stayed in touch with me. Not often but every once in a while she calls. The last time was when Vincent came to see her."

"Where is she now?" Mickey asked.

"She wouldn't tell me. I only get calls from her."

"Have you told us everything now?" I asked.

"Yes."

"Everything that you told Vincent?"

"Yes."

I was sure that was all we were going to get out of her. I said, "We've taken enough of your time. Thanks for your help." Mickey and I got up.

"I told you everything," Barbara said.

"I believe you," I said. This time I did. "I do have another question, though."

"What is it?"

"You seem to have changed your life-style recently."

"What do you mean?"

"I mean the move from an apartment into this new house. The new car outside. The new furniture on order..."

She smiled. A genuine smile. A materialistic smile. "Yes. Clyde finally got the money from his mother's will. Those lawyers can drag it out forever."

"That's why they bill by the hour," I said.

We thanked her again and started to leave. "One last thing," I added. "The police will be looking for you because of Gutman. If they find you, tell them the truth about Vincent. But don't mention the army investigation. It's a question of jurisdiction."

Inside the car, I said, "So Gutman had a Nevada lead on his daughter in March and in April the body count started. Obviously, he tracked her down through one of these names Barbara gave him."

"Let's hope we do as well," Mickey said. "This time I believed her," she added as I pulled away from the curb.

I drove out past a row of Quail Point model homes. Red pennants were flapping over a huge sign that advertised the current prices. Expensive.

"What now?" Mickey asked.

"I've got to call Johnny D. and tell him what we found out."

Before I reached the highway I spotted a pizza place where we could get lunch and I could telephone Johnny. It was one of the better chains that claimed to use real cheese and real tomatoes. We agreed on a Sicilian-style pizza and beer for me, wine for Mickey.

"Gutman is alive," I said.

"Confirmed how?" Johnny asked.

"Phone contact."

"Who did he call?"

"His ex-wife. She's remarried." I gave him the name and address.

"All right. We'll get out an APB on Gutman. Thanks, Jeremiah. Keep in touch." He said and hung up.

An All Points Bulletin. Sounded impressive but it doesn't always get results. Still my conscience was clear.

Next I called the office and left a message for the Chief with some very specific instructions. There was a good chance I would need his contacts in Nevada. The only person I couldn't reach was Nancy. There was no answer at her home.

When I got back to our table, the pizza was already there. Fast. Just as the ads on TV promised.

"So on to Nevada." I poured my beer into a pilsner glass.

Mickey stopped chewing her pizza. "I know. But I forgot to break my tennis date with Glenn tonight."

"There's the phone."

She checked her watch. "I won't be able to reach him now."

"Business before pleasure. Or even tennis." I bit into the thick, chewy crust.

When I had finished my second piece and started a third, I signaled for another beer.

She picked at her first piece of pizza but drank the rest of her wine. "I lost my appetite."

"Why?" I asked.

"This whole thing makes me apprehensive. A serial killer, for God's sake."

"Me too." Small consolation.

I paid the check and we headed out. The easy route was to go as directly as possible to Interstate 80 for the run to Tahoe. But every once in a while I got the urge to do the back roads of California. Especially in perfect weather like this. So I took the country roads through the delta, passing lazy riverboats and islands that seemed to float by on the water. We crossed the San Joaquin at Rio Vista and drove through the orchards of western Solano County. The rural road came to an abrupt end at Travis Air Force Base. That brought us to 80. From there it took us three hours, across the great central valley, up into the high Sierras, to Lake Tahoe—a lake so large and deep it contains enough water to cover the entire state at a depth of fourteen inches. Or to satisfy the insatiable water demands of Los Angeles for a couple of days. We exited at Truckee and drove past ski resorts and condo villages. At 7,000 feet we went over a summit and Carnelian Bay was below us, a deep blue facet of the Tahoe sapphire.

"Beautiful, isn't it?"

"Where do we have reservations?" Mickey asked.

"Consider it a surprise."

"I can't wait."

I continued east along the rim of the lake for about two miles until we crossed into Nevada at Crystal Bay. In front of us was the Silver Bar Casino, straddling the state line.

"Not there?" she asked, pointing to the hotel attached to the casino.

"Too obvious." I drove on.

Ten minutes later we were in Incline Village at the entrance to the Tahoe Tennis and Ski Lodge.

"You're obsessed," Mickey said.

"That's what makes me good at my job."

9

Rising above the lodge, tennis courts, and a parking lot were a dozen blue flags waving in a light breeze. I drove under them through the lot to the front of the lodge and parked in a space marked Guest Registration.

"I've got to call Glenn," she said. "He'll need another doubles partner."

"I'm sure he'll come up with one. Maybe one of his many ex-wives."

We went into the lodge. There was a huge black-metal fireplace in the center of the lobby with sofas and chairs spread out around it. Right now there was no fire burning, but I knew that tonight it would be cold enough for one. The decor combined alpine skiing and flatland tennis. The walls were covered with photographs and posters of male and female stars of both sports and with crossed old-fashioned wooden skis and wooden rackets. Tennis and ski magazines were scattered on the tables between the sofas and chairs. We were at the transition point between spring skiing and spring tennis.

The clerk behind the registration desk had a full white beard. He was still into winter in a heavy ski sweater, red trimmed with white. He could have passed for a California-style Santa Claus— healthily trim.

The lodge only had apartments and I had made our reservations for a two-bedroom with a view. Sometimes I do things with the proper grace.

I carried our suitcases into the apartment, which occupied a third-story corner of the lodge. Between the bedrooms—each with a private bath—was a living room with a stone fireplace, beamed ceilings, redwood paneling, plush wall-to-wall carpeting in beige, and a private balcony that held a generous stack of firewood. There was a modern tile-and-oak kitchen, with a new stove, a microwave, and a refrigerator with an ice maker. The Tahoe Tennis and Ski Lodge sat high enough on a plateau so that most of the lake was visible below it. From the balcony, through a veil of ponderosa pine, we had a spectacular view of the azure waters. In the distance, the mountains rimming the lake were powdered with the snow that brought out the spring ski bunnies in their bikinis, shorts, and sometimes even topless. We could hear a creek outside, running down through the pines into Tahoe, a lake that depended entirely on snowfall and runoff for water.

The surroundings soothed the lady. She stretched out on the couch in the living room. "It is beautiful," she said.

I called the Nevada DMV with Jackie's birth date. No luck. With the California border so close, some of the casino workers lived there—though Nevada was better for tax purposes. I gave California a try. No luck there, either.

Mickey went out on the balcony. "I can see the courts from here," she said as she leaned precariously around the corner of the building. "They look great."

"They're some of the best."

"What's next?" she asked as she came back in.

Next was a call to the Silver Bar Casino. I asked for Opal Chesko.

"She don't come on again till tomorrow at eight," a male voice informed me in a New Jersey accent.

"Eight at night?" I asked.

"Nah. She got the day shift."

They must have imported this guy from Atlantic City for atmosphere.

"What about a Sherry Wine? A dancer?" I asked.

He had to think aout it. "She's still here. But she's off until Friday."

I thanked the voice and hung up.

"We have a shot," I said to Mickey. "But we have to wait until tomorrow morning at least."

There was nothing else left to do but enjoy what the lodge had to offer. We stopped at the pro shop, where Mickey bought a tennis dress, Nike tennis shoes, and rented a Prince racket. Since we were at about 6,500 feet, I bought a can of high-altitude tennis balls for the thin air.

We had a light meal courtside—at a glass-topped table under a sun umbrella—at the Set Point Cafe. I laid off the beer. This was serious tennis.

A half hour later we were changed and out on the courts. I remembered one of the things I liked about tennis when I saw Mickey in her new tennis dress with a scoop neck and a tiny skirt that barely covered her white tennis panties. She would be a great distraction in a mixed doubles match.

The courts were a little bit different from those in Lafayette Park. The green and red hard surface had no chips or cracks in it. There were no holes in these nets. Every court was separated from the one next to it by a walkway, flower beds of Shasta daisies, and crushed stone borders. No cramming together here. There were water fountains, benches, tables, and courtside shade. An intercom put you in contact with the outdoor bar, which employed a dozen ball girls in appropriate costumes—except that the shorts were modified to look like the hot pants of the seventies—eager to deliver.

We had a session with a young club pro, who had a Rastafarian hairdo that made him look like Yannick Noah. During our session, he corrected three errors in mechanics for me and declared Mickey to be just about perfect. I could have told him that.

After an early dinner in the lodge and a rest, we played under the lights against another couple for two exhausting hours. It was getting alpine cold and we were all getting tired but we persisted. We won the third and final set when our male opponent looked at Mickey bending over (to prepare to volley) right in front of him instead of at the ball I had hit to him. He missed it completely.

"Nice play on match point," I whispered to Mickey.

"I was freezing," she said.

As we hurried back to the lodge I said, "I'll light a fire back in the apartment."

"Don't get any Jim Morrison ideas."

"No way. After all that tennis, we need our separate rooms," I admitted. "Not music by The Doors."

"And separate Jacuzzis."

"And separate ice packs," I muttered. Now that the adrenaline had stopped pumping, I suddenly felt like I needed to ice down at least a dozen muscles and joints.

"You really have gotten much better," Mickey said. "And in such a short time."

"My muscles are getting their memory back. Only thing is, it's killing them."

As I unlocked the door Mickey blurted out, "Damn. I forgot to call Glenn."

Mr. St. John: fifteen; Dr. Earnhard: love. It didn't sound right, but that's how you kept score in tennis.

We went to our rooms and collapsed. I never did bother to light a fire.

Somewhere a phone was ringing. Somewhere in my head. I sat up. No. It was somewhere in the room. On the night table. I reached over and knocked the receiver off. It was the goddamn wake-up call I had requested.

As I retrieved it a chirpy voice gave me the time and hung up with a "Good morning and good tennis!"

I slammed the receiver down and covered my head with my pillow. I wanted to go back to sleep. But I knew better.

I called our answering machine and activated it with my code. The Chief had taken action on the message I had recorded after we talked to Barbara Shatts. He had left the words: "The fort is captured." He had made the right connections with his Nevada contacts. I had an ace up my sleeve.

I could hear Mickey's shower going. I dressed and waited in the living room with the morning paper—a rag full of nothing—until Mickey appeared in her tennis outfit.

"I'm going to sign up for the A-level class this morning," she said. "I assume you don't need me at the casino."

"Not this time."

"We forgot to shop for food," she said, grinning.

"I know."

It was back to the Set Point Cafe. Afterwards, she went off to class and I went to the parking lot. I drove back to the state line and parked at the Silver Bar Casino. Unlike the Vegas scene, the early morning crowd at Tahoe was always light. Too many other activities besides gambling. It would be a good time for talking to Opal Chesko.

I went into the casino, past the bright colored lights of the slot machines that robbed you blind no matter what the ads said about payoffs, past the glowing screens of the video poker games, to the tables. Where the real gamblers played.

Most of the action this early was at the slots. Players left over from last night who hadn't realized it was a new day. One of the reasons there are no clocks in casinos.

An alarm went off, a red light began to turn on top of a slot machine, and silver dollars poured musically out. A nice haul but I was sure the sucker would wind up feeding it all back into the machine.

There was no one playing roulette or shooting craps. I wandered past the croupiers to the blackjack tables. Two bored young women in black slacks and white blouses were standing behind two empty kidney-shaped tables waiting for some action. A third woman was at the five-dollar table dealing to two men, one a guy about my age with curly blond hair, the other a Japanese who could have been sixteen or sixty. I checked the gold nameplates the women wore. Opal was dong the dealing.

She didn't look the way I expected. She was a slight woman of about thirty with straight black hair to her shoulders, moonstone fair skin, and delicate if somewhat sharp features. Her eyes were large, dark, and mischievous, and her thin lips were slightly curled in one corner, giving her a cynical look. She had the high cheek-bones of a model but not the height. I took the third-base stool to be right next to her.

Blackjack, where the odds are least in favor of the house, is my favorite casino game. I pulled out my wallet.

Opal held up the game while I cashed a hundred-dollar bill for five-dollar chips, which she pushed in two neat stacks across the green felt to me.

Neither man acknowledged my presence. A sure sign they were losing.

Two hands later the Japanese man sitting at first base was joined by his wife. On the next hand he lost fifty dollars on a pair of split aces and the couple left. I heard the woman asking him for more money. I didn't hear his answer.

Opal looked after them and shook her head. He hadn't left a tip.

Now there were two of us plus Opal. The blond guy was sitting to my right in the center seat. He was thin, with the drawn, lined face of a heavy smoker. He was wearing an expensive suit so wrinkled, it looked like he had been rolling around on the casino floor in it. He lit up a cigarette. I noticed that there was a SMOKING sign on Opal's table. I looked around. On some of the other tables there were NO SMOKING signs. Even to me they seemed incongruous in a casino.

Blondy lost with seventeen and I had a push.

"Damn, I shoulda taken that card. I woulda had twenty-one." He was looking at my four which had given me eighteen which matched the house hand.

I shrugged.

"Don't whine," Opal said to him.

"Huh?" he asked in surprise.

"No whining," she repeated.

"I dropped a bundle this week," he whined.

She shook her head and dealt. She was like no dealer I had ever run across in my life.

I held at sixteen and Blondy went bust. Opal had to hit at sixteen and she busted with a King.

"Damn," she said.

Opal was different. That was the first time I had heard a dealer express any concern whether the house won or lost.

I smiled as I scooped in the winnings on a twenty-five-dollar bet.

"I shoulda held," Blondy complained.

Opal just shook her head again. I wished Blondy would go broke. I had some investigating to do. Still, I couldn't complain. I was up over two hundred dollars. The nice thing about charging expenses to a client is that if you have a necessary gambling loss, the client pays. If you win, it's your bonus. A perk.

Three hands later Opal dealt me my first blackjack.

"Why don't you deal me blackjack, honey?" Blondy said as he lit up another cigarette. "'Stead a him?"

"Because he's cute, honey!"

Blondy shut up.

I checked his pile of chips. If he didn't put in some new money, the way he was playing, he'd be gone in a couple of hands.

While Opal was shuffling the decks in the shoe a cocktail waitress wearing a very skimpy outfit asked Blondy and me if we wanted drinks. It was a little too early for me. But Blondy ordered a Bloody Mary.

Before it arrived, Blondy was broke and gone, without leaving a tip.

"Good riddance," Opal said.

"Not very good at the game."

"You ought to give him some lessons. He was taking hits at seventeen when I'm showing fourteen or fifteen. He even split a pair of kings. And then lost on both hands."

Blondy's Bloody Mary came. The waitress looked around for him.

I put a chip on her dish and took the drink. It was later than before and all of my muscles were starting to remind me about the hours of tennis last night. I hoped the Bloody Mary would help.

Since there were just the two of us, I slowed the game down, taking my time to decide on hits or holds, to make conversation. When I got worried that a new dealer would be stepping in shortly to replace her, I got to the point.

"I knew a dealer here once. A Jackie Gutman. You know her?"

"No."

"You sure?" I tipped her four five-dollar chips on my winning hand.

"I don't know her," she said as she dealt out new cards.

I took a hit at thirteen and drew a King. "That's not what I hear." I passed four more chips to her on my busted hand.

"Tell me. You need to find her because she's been left a million dollars in a long-lost relative's will."

"Not exactly. But I am trying to help her."

"Help her by leaving her alone."

"Do you get off for lunch?"

"Yeah."

"How about having it with me?" I asked.

"Sure. Why not? Make up for lost tips. Meet me at the lunch place across the street at noon," she said.

That was fine with me. She was replaced by a young man with bushy red hair and a freckled face. I stayed for a half dozen quick hands and left at noon.

The place across the street was an ersatz log cabin across the state line in California. I could tell because there were no slot machines or video poker games packed in by the entrance.

I sat down in a booth and looked at the menu while I waited. The house specialty was chicken, made in any of fifteen different ways. A waitress in a white outfit that made her look like an over-sexed nurse asked if I was ready to order. I was surprised that she wasn't wearing a San Diego Chicken suit instead.

"I'm waiting for someone. But I'll have a Henry Weinhard's.

"What's that?"

"A beer."

"We don't got it. We got Coors and Bud on tap."

I settled for Bud in honor of the Chief.

My beer and Opal arrived simultaneously. She ordered an iced tea and said, "I have to keep the cards straight this afternoon."

"What do you recommend?" I asked.

"The chicken."

"No kidding."

"Go with the barbecued. The sauce is great."

We both ordered barbecued chicken. I got a leg, a thigh, and a breast. Opal just ordered a single piece.

I gave it another try on Jackie. "About Jackie Gutman. You don't deny knowing her."

"She used to work here."

"And now?"

"I don't know."

"It sounded like you were trying to protect her before."

"Did it?"

"Yes, it did," I insisted.

"You're wrong."

"Anyone else asking abut Jackie lately?" I tried.

She hesitated. "No."

"You sure? How about back in March?"

"No one asked me."

I took out a copy of the composite drawing of Vincent Gutman and showed it to her. "Somebody who looks like this."

She ignored the picture. "No one asked about her. Understand?"

I understood enough to stop asking. We still had Sherry Wine to talk to.

Opal took a bite of her chicken. I was down to the thigh. The barbecue sauce was good. I ordered another Bud, another iced tea, and some more barbecue sauce. After that we just made small talk. Opal tore into the tourist gamblers and most anything else from the road salt used in winter that was killing the pines around the lake, to the drought that was lowering its level, to the sediment from construction sites that was ruining the perfect clarity of the lake.

"Right now you can still see the bottom at depths of 150 feet. But we're losing it every year."

I appreciated the environmental lecture but I did have other things on my mind.

I paid the check and walked her across the street.

"Aren't you coming in?" she asked.

"Can't," I said.

"Are you a private investigator?"

"Good guess."

"Leave Jackie alone."

"If you want to talk about Jackie, here's my card." I took out an agency card and wrote my Tahoe number on it.

She took the card and opened her purse, took out a pen and pad, and wrote down a phone number. "Give me a call if you want to talk about anything else."

I laughed and took the phone number. I got into the T-Bird and drove off, leaving her standing in front of the casino entrance, looking at my card like it was a bad check.

Back at the Tahoe Tennis and Ski Lodge, I explained to a hot, tired, and sunburned Mickey that I had struck out with Opal and that it was now her time to try with Sherry Wine.

"Mickey, let me fill you in on the Chief's connections and my plan"

She listened carefully and said, "Then we have some equipment to rent."

We had to drive to South Lake Tahoe to rent what we needed and get some business cards printed for our cover.

Friday morning after breakfast we drove Mickey to the Silver Bar Casino. She was dressed appropriately in a loose striped T-shirt, jeans, and her tennis shoes.

The casino must have been unusually crowded and we had to park in an underground lot behind it. As we walked to the entrance Mickey said, "I hope this works."

"Trust me," I said as I handed over to her the video equipment we had rented. "We have the word of the Chief on it."

We avoided the casino and Opal and went right into the nightclub area. On stage, six young women in a rainbow of leotards and tights were running through a dance routine. A pale young man with stringy black hair was pounding out the music on an old concert grand. He was wearing a T-shirt that read "Please Don't Shoot the Piano Player" on the back.

Mickey and I stood in the back watching. The director was standing in front of the stage with his back to us. The choreography looked basic.

The music stopped and I led Mickey and her video camera down through the empty tables to the man in charge. The director was a red-faced Irishman named Joe Coglin. He was in his fifties and looked it. His gray hair was mostly gone, his skin was mottled, his eyes bloodshot, and his jowls heavy. There was an unlit cigar tucked into the corner of his mouth. He wore an extra-large University of Nevada Las Vegas Running Rebels sweatshirt and matching sweatpants. For equal time, he had on a Nevada-Reno baseball cap. He didn't look like he could dance a box step much less choreograph one.

He looked at Mickey and asked, "Yeah? Whaddya want?"

I introduced myself and handed him a card that indicated I was from the North Tahoe Tourism Bureau. "We have an opportunity here for some free TV publicity," I said, pointing to Mickey and her camera equipment.

"We don't need it," he said.

"Michelle here is from '*California Video Magazine*.' You've heard of that TV interview show, I'm sure. Carried all over both states. She's here to do a feature on a showgirl's life in North Tahoe. With plugs for the casino and North Tahoe. The Tourism Bureau loves it."

"I don't belong to the Bureau and I don't give a shit about what they love. Now take a hike with that equipment."

Sometimes you go with the hard sell. I took out a St. John Agency business car and handed it to him. He studied it, looked at me, looked at Mickey, bit his lower lip, and finally nodded.

Mickey smiled at him.

"Well, we could use some free publicity," Coglin said meekly. "Whaddya need from me?"

"Good. That's the spirit we like at the NTTB. She needs tape of their rehearsals and performances and she needs to interview at least one of the dancers." I lowered my voice and added, "And her cover kept intact."

"No problem. She's from TV. That's all I know."

"Your cooperation is noted," I said.

There was a look of relief on Coglin's face.

"But I need to ask you a few questions."

The look of relief passed.

"Did you know Jackie Gutman?"

"She a dancer?"

"A dealer."

"Must have been before I moved here from South Tahoe."

I showed him the Gutman picture.

"Yeah. He was around here. What? Last month. Bugging the girls. I had him thrown out."

"Did he stay away?"

"I didn't see him."

"Any girl in particular?"

"Sherry Wine," he said emphatically.

I looked at Mickey. We had a lead.

I thanked Coglin and left Mickey to her work while I went back to the blackjack tables. Opal was nowhere in sight so I settled into a twenty-five dollar minimum-bet game at one of the No Smoking tables.

Two hours later I won a hundred-dollar bet on a pair of split eights, which left me several hundred up for the afternoon. I tipped the dealer and headed back to the nightclub area.

Mickey was sitting on the edge of the stage talking to Coglin. When she saw me, she got up and walked over to me.

"Will you haul out the equipment?" she asked.

"Anything for show business."

"Let's get out of here."

I put the equipment into the trunk and Mickey into the front seat. "Well, how'd it go?" I asked.

"I'm starving."

"Did you get to talk to Sherry Wine?"

"No."

"Did you get some good tape at least?" I asked.

"I was crawling all over the stage getting angles on the dancers. I must have something."

"So the showgirls bought your story?"

"I worked hard enough at it."

"Good job. First show's at eight."

"I can hardly wait," she muttered.

We had time to go to a supermarket in Incline and go back to the apartment for dinner.

Back in the car, Mickey said, "The Chief did a good job. I loved the look on Coglin's face when you gave him our agency card. He has been very polite."

"Contacts matter." The Chief had talked to Tommy Dong who talked to a man who talked to Joe Coglin.

After rare steaks, baked potatoes with sour cream and chives and salad, Mickey had her strength back. I waited while she changed into something a little less casual and then we drove back to the casino.

Mickey went backstage with her camcorder and I got myself a table up front with a ten spot and managed to get a Henry's. The show was unimaginatively called *Las Vegas Revue*. Maybe it sounded big time for Tahoe. It started with a female torch singer in a melted-on red dress. Her voice was pretty good, too. The girls came out for their first number wearing chartreuse feather plumes on their heads, fancy paste diamonds around their necks, black fishnet stockings on their legs, and pink spiked heels on their feet. And not much more than oversized pasties, modified G-strings, and a few strategically placed tail feathers—all in chartreuse and pink.

They did several elaborate routines, including a final topless number that made the show look Vegas. The headliner followed. He was a decent comedian who kept a poker face while cracking jokes at both his and the audience's expense.

Another bottle of beer later the first show was over. There was no sign of Mickey. I took a break and threw some money away at the craps tables. Very good odds for the player, too, but I never seem to win at it. At ten o'clock I sat down for the second show. Halfway through the first number Mickey appeared at my table.

"Let's get out of here," she said.

I left my bottle of Henry's unfinished and picked up her video gear. We drove back to the lodge.

"How'd it go, Michelle," I said.

"Don't call me Michelle, Jerry! I hate it!"

"Okay. Truce," I said. The last person to call me Jerry was a sleazy P.I. named Leo Stubbs who wound up in jail. "Did you get a chance to talk to Sherry?"

"Yes. She's the tall brunette with the long face on the extreme right of the line. I brought up Jackie Gutman between shows. I said I used to know her in Pittsburg back in high school. I think Sherry knows something but I have to go slow."

"Seems to be the rule around here."

I was driving along Lakeshore, past huge houses and grand estates lit up like castles in the starry night. By the time I stopped at the blinking red light in front of the Hyatt Hotel and Casino, Mickey was sound asleep.

I walked with a very groggy Mickey into our lodge apartment. She promptly sat down on the couch and fell asleep again. I got her into bed with a modest minimum of undressing and called Johnny D. at home. The April Fool Killer had made good on his promise to strike on the twenty-ninth. We had another victim.

"Nevada connection?" I asked.

"A loose one. His wife said he made a trip to Reno recently."

"Any connection to Stein and the other victims?"

"We haven't been able to link any of 'em."

"But you don't believe it's random?" I asked.

"No. You gotta go to Nevada to qualify."

"Not just Nevada. Reno. None of these guys went to Vegas."

"What am I supposed to do with that, Jeremiah?"

"Whatever cops do with information. Point it out to Chang."

"Thanks."

"The other victims were single," I added.

"Yeah. So?"

"I don't know. What did this guy do?" I asked.

"Sold Hondas."

"And I thought they had high owner satisfaction."

Johnny hung up but not before reminding me what tomorrow was: Saturday, April 30. The day the next random Nevada victim was scheduled to die.

I called Nancy. She knew all about the murder. I told her that Vincent had called Barbara.

"I was right. He's alive."

"And killing tourists who visit Reno."

"Please find him," she pleaded.

"I'm following the only lead I have. A connection to Jackie in Nevada. "

"How's that going?" she asked.

"Slowly." It was the truth.

10

Much as I hated to do it, Saturday morning I packed to leave. I couldn't be sure if I could ever get anything out of Opal and I didn't know how long it would take Mickey to get anything useful out of Sherry Wine. And I didn't want Opal to connect me with Mickey and possibly warn Sherry. Besides, if I was going to keep my word to Nancy and find Gutman, I had to get back to San Francisco, where he was most likely to be. Privately, I was rooting for the SFPD and their APB to get to Vincent first, but I had to give it my professional best.

I woke Mickey up as gently as I could and explained the situation.

She sat up. The sheet and blanket were drawn up to her chin.

First, she didn't appreciate being awakened at whatever ungodly hour it was in the morning. Second, she didn't appreciate being abandoned in Tahoe without transportation. Third, she didn't like being abandoned at all.

I explained the situation again. Slowly.

She fell back on her pillow.

"I'll leave you the T-Bird," I said.

She sat up again. "What? Your beloved classic? One of the only two true American sports cars ever produced?"

"Yes."

"I'm moved."

"Me too. Right out of here."

"Not so fast, partner."

"What's the problem?"

"I need some operating instructions."

"Sure," I said.

"I depress the clutch to shift, right?"

"That's the usual procedure. If you want to keep the gears intact. But come on. You've driven the T-Bird before."

"Sure. Remember that high-speed chase?"

I did. It gave me a funny feeling in my stomach. Maybe this
generous act on my part was a dumb idea.

"Just no high-speed chases along the rim of the lake," I pleaded.

"Only if absolutely necessary," she promised.

"Boy, am I relieved to hear that."

"What if something goes wrong?" she asked.

"The Chief just tuned it up."

"But it's not exactly brand new," she insisted.

"There's an owner's manual in the glove compartment."

"You're joking."

"Call AAA if you have a problem on the road."

"I'm not a member."

"Now you are." I gave her my AAA card.

"What about insurance? I have to have insurance."

"Here." I gave her my California Proof of Insurance Card.

"Gasoline?"

I gave her my Union 76 credit card.

"Anything else?"

"The keys, Jeremiah. It would be like you to walk out with them
after all this."

It wouldn't have been bad passive-aggressive behavior. Or a kind
of Freudian slip designed to save my car.

"Here are the keys." I tossed them to her.

"All right, go," she said as she snagged them in midair and almost lost the top of the sheet covering her.

"You almost joined the topless revue," I said. "Call as soon as
you learn anything about Jackie."

"No. I'm going to stay up here until I get everything I need for
the video magazine."

I kissed her good-bye on the cheek.

As I moved to the door Mickey said, "Thanks for last night."

"Huh?"

"For putting me to bed modesty intact."

I gave a casual shrug. "You seem pretty naked under there now."

"I am. I woke up in the middle of the night, stripped, and showered."

"Well, since you're so appropriately undressed..."

She threw the feather pillow at me.

I caught the pillow and tossed it back to her. "Go to sleep. You need the rest."

Suddenly she started up in bed, losing and recovering the sheet as her cover in a flash second. "I forgot to call Glenn! It's all your fault."

"Too late. You stood him up. Left him to the consolations of his ex-wives." I grabbed my gear and was out the door. Something harder than a pillow exploded against the wood as I shut it.

I had given the T-Bird to Mickey as a peace offering for leaving her up here alone without thinking of my travel options. Now I needed a phone. But I decided not to go back into the condo. I didn't want to give Mickey a chance to change her mind.

I went into the lodge and the desk clerk told me about Cal-Neva Airlines, a single-plane operation. He got them on the phone. It turned out that they had a seaplane going to the Bay Area and room for one more passenger. "Cost you a hundred dollars cash and you gotta be ready to go in a half hour," the pilot and owner of the operation told me. I arranged to be picked up at the dock of the Hyatt Hotel, which I could walk to in about ten minutes. I headed downhill to the lake.

Fifteen minutes later I saw the plane approaching from the direction of its Homewood base. It hit the water on amphibian floats and taxied up to the dock. The plane's door opened and the pilot, who looked to be in his late sixties, let down a ladder. I climbed up into the single-engine deHaviland Beaver, modified to function as a seaplane. Perfect for a commute from Lake Tahoe to San Francisco Bay.

I took one of the five empty seats—a window seat—and put my

gear behind it. The pilot collected my money in cash and taxied away from the dock.

"Any other passengers?" I shouted over the roar of the engine.

He didn't answer. We bounced along on the chop until we lifted off the lake. Five minutes later we landed and taxied up to a dock attached to one of the modern palaces on Lakeshore Drive. There were four men waiting for the plane. All of them wore dark suits, had pencil-thin mustaches, and were chained to attaché cases. Very inconspicuous.

"Who are these guys?" I shouted to the pilot while we were still a few feet from the dock.

This time he heard me. "Casino people. Don't ask anything else. You don't want to know. And I don't recommend any small talk with them," he shouted.

"I have a window seat. I'll enjoy the view."

"Good idea."

The pilot repeated the docking procedure and loaded the plane. Nobody said anything. He slammed the door shut, collected his money, and taxied away from the dock. Several bumpy minutes later we were airborne.

I spent the entire trip looking out the window. My traveling companions sat in silence and stared straight ahead. They didn't know or care what they were missing. Unlike the view from a commercial airliner there was a lot to see from this much-lower altitude. We left the mountain-ringed bowl of Tahoe behind, rose above the ice blue of Donner Lake, climbed over the snowcapped Sierras, and then dropped down into the vast central valley. The pilot followed the black ribbon of Interstate 80, going over Sacramento, with its golden Capitol dome clearly visible from the air, and arriving at our first destination, a seaplane base by Sausalito, after a mere sixty-five minutes in the air. I was the only one who got off there.

"Enjoy the rest of the trip, gentlemen," I said as I climbed down the ladder. They didn't answer. "Anyone willing to cover a bet on the A's getting into the World Series this year?" No answer. "How about the Forty-Niners winning the Super Bowl?"

"Hey, fuck you, wiseass!" one of them finally said.

"So you're not going to a convention of mutes," I shouted as the pilot pulled up the ladder and slammed the door shut before anyone had a chance to consider pushing me off the dock. That was fine with me.

I took my bag and racket into the metal shed that served as base headquarters. If the Chief was at the office, it would only be a twenty-minute ride at this time of day to come out and get me. I looked around. Against the back wall there was a battered wooden desk covered with an old-fashioned blotter and piles of papers. An ashtray full of butts sat square in the middle of it like a paperweight. Next to the desk there was a metal filing cabinet, the color of weak mustard, with the lock broken off. In a corner of the room there was a radio setup for ground-to-air communications. There was a single rest-room door that had a sign on it that read MEN Under that sign was a piece of cardboard on which someone had written in block letters: WOMEN TOO. Whoever was in charge must have been in the unisex john, although I had my suspicions that the door just led right to the bay outside. The thing I was looking for, however, I didn't see—an office phone. I settled for the pay phone hanging on the wall and got Chief Moses before the man in charge showed up.

A half hour later I was in his pickup truck heading back to Octavia Street. His driving reminded me of what Mickey could be doing in my T-Bird. I shuddered. Chief Moses turned down the air-conditioning in response.

I filled him in on Mickey's current undercover role.

"Will the woman be safe?" he asked.

"I don't see why not. She has Dong's clout behind her, a solid cover, my T-bird, and her custom gun."

The Chief nodded. "She is a pro." He went on to tell me that there had been more telephone threats to Dong's poker parlors but no overt actions. The pressure was on him to pay off. The Yellow Suns were watching all of the parlors, setting the trap, while the Chief was working on the juror profiles.

"I would be further along on them if I did not have to drive around a detective who lost his car."

"It was a loan."

"She will probably sell it."

"She doesn't have the papers."

The Chief looked blank. "Who needs papers?"

Half a block away from the office, the Chief struggled to squeeze the pickup into a small space. One final turn of the wheel, one final twist of the neck, one last grunt, one final rap against the bumper of the late-model Pontiac behind him and he was in.

It was lunchtime but there was nothing that didn't look and smell moldy in my refrigerator. I left the Chief doing his paperwork and went out the grocery store on Sutter. The place was owned and operated by three Vietnamese brothers named Chew who came to America as boat people.

I walked under the green canvas awning, past the open crates of fresh fruits and vegetables over which hung a hand-lettered sign that read CERTIFIED PESTICIDE FREE.

In the window on a bed of crushed ice rested several large whole fish I couldn't identify. I avoided their glassy eyes as I entered the store.

I went over to the deli counter manned by the brother who liked to be called Hank after Henry Aaron. I heard the A's playing the Cleveland Indians (one of the teams whose name and logo, along with those of the Atlanta Braves and the Washington Redskins, offended the Chief) on the radio on the counter behind him. The Chews were all avid baseball fans.

I ordered a pound of sliced smoked turkey, a pound of rare roast beef, and half pound of Swiss cheese, two huge kosher dill pickles, and a bucket of potato salad. The only thing not moldy in the refrigerator was beer, of which there was plenty. I picked up a jar of hot mustard, a jar of roasted sliced red peppers, and a loaf of sourdough French bread.

As Hank was counting out my change he asked, "You are Mr. St. John, that detective?"

"Yes."

"I read about you in Vietnamese newspaper."

"No kidding." I was impressed with myself.

"Said you solved murder case."

"That was a while ago."

"Talk to you in private?" he asked.

"Okay, Hank."

He led me back into a small storeroom and turned on the single overhead light bulb. I was surrounded by precariously stacked cases of canned goods that went all the way up to the ceiling. I hoped this was not the moment for the big earthquake to hit. I didn't want to come to my end crushed by a case of canned peaches in the back room of an Asian grocery store. I had more romantic visions of Jeremiah St. John's grand departure.

"We have been getting threats."

"What kind?"

"To pay for protection. They call it insurance. Fire insurance."

"The threat of arson if you don't pay off."

"You have got it, Mr. St. John."

"Anything happen to the store yet?"

"No. Not yet."

"Did you call the police?"

"They say not to call police."

"That's what they always say. These guys actually came around here? You saw them?"

"One. We see one of them."

"Was he Vietnamese?"

"No. American. Thin. With beard. Dress like soldier. Act like soldier. Even spoke some Vietnamese."

I knew a few men like that.

"He say he be back to get money."

"When?"

"Not say."

"Did you tell him you would pay off?"

"We not say anything to him. You help us?"

I thought it over. There were obvious similarities to the Dong case. "Okay. I'll see what I can do. But there will be some expenses."

"Hank" Chew nodded gravely.

Back at the office over sandwiches and beer I told the Chief about Hank Chew's story and he said, "I would call Tran Van Dam. But his men are stretched thin watching the poker parlors."

"You're right. I know some other men I can use."

"One case may solve the other. Like a second arrow shot to find the first that was lost," he said.

"Old Indian saying?"

"Shakespeare. *Merchant of Venice.*"

"I thought it sounded familiar."

He got up to leave. "I have work to do. We need those juror profiles done."

After the Chief left, I called Johnny D.

"What now?" he asked.

"Anybody hitting on Vietnamese businesses?"

"What? We got a murder last night and another one threatened for tonight. The April Fool Killer is running wild in the city and you want to know about what—some petty extortion attempts? Christ."

"There might be a connection to the April Fool Killer," I offered.

He sighed. "That would be Bunco."

"I don't have a contact there. Would you check on it?"

"I ain't in your employ."

"You never know. Someday you might be. We have a lot of ex-cops in this business. I have one beautiful one myself." Then I repeated the same bait line: "Might be a connection to the April Fool Killer." Maybe. Maybe not. But this time Johnny took it like a shark.

"Are we talkin' Asian gangs here? We got those up the ol' whazoo."

"No. Whites."

"How 'bout Hispanics. They could look white an' we got lots of 'em."

"No. Whites. Pink skins." I hoped the Chews knew the difference.

"Whites, huh. All right. I'll look into it." He hung up. Man can I get action.

I went through the office lock-up routine and headed for California Street. I took the cable car to Powell, where I switched lines to get me closer to the Tenderloin. The cable car dropped me off two blocks east of the Dragon Seeds headquarters.

Curtis was in the outer room playing chess with another black man. The rest of the men were playing cards. All of them were smoking. With the lack of ventilation, breathing normally had to be the equivalent of smoking a pack of unfiltered Camels.

"You wanted some P.I. work," I said to Curtis, "you got some."

"Not for me, man. Got all I can handle. From some a the vets."

"You hear of any white gangs hitting on Vietnamese stores?"'

"White?"'

"Yeah."

"Not Hispanic?"'

"Pink skins."

"No. Why you askin' me, man?"'

"Vets may be involved."

"You sure?"'

"No. But one of these guys could speak some Vietnamese. I don't think he picked it up at a language course at SF State."

"Makes sense. Only white ones?"' He blew smoke into the air.

"Who the hell knows, Curtis. There are white guys out on the point on this."

"Didn't help you much with Gutman so far," he said.

"So try this."

He coughed. "I gotta give up them cancer sticks."

"Will you try, Curtis?"'

He coughed again. "Exactly what you want?"'

I explained the Chew grocery situation to him.

Curtis whistled and got everyone's attention. He announced, "This man gonna make you an offer."

I repeated what I had told Curtis, stressing that we were dealing with a gang of whites. "I'm going to need men for a twenty-four-hour undercover surveillance. That would be six on four-hour shifts. All of you will be inside the store. During the day you'll be posing as customers. During the night you can sleep if you're a light sleeper. If not, stay awake. I figure whoever it is will hit soon and while the store is open. Probably at the end of the day when there's the most cash in the registers. But there's a chance they'll try to intimidate them first with some kind of vandalism."

"What's the pay scale?"'

"Minimum wage."

"Shee-it," Agent Orange announced as he crushed out a cigarette and immediately lit another one.

I threw in a fringe benefit I would have to sell to Hank and his brothers. "You get a free meal at the deli."

"All I can eat?"' the large Agent Orange asked.

"Sure," I said, hoping I would not bankrupt the Chew brothers.

I ended up hiring Agent Orange and five other men for the job.

"When do we start?" they asked through a fog of gray second-hand smoke.

I told them to wait until I called.

I made another cash contribution to the Dragon Seeds.

I asked Curtis to come outside.

"Check," he said to his opponent as he moved his black Queen and got up.

The city's street air seemed alpine clean compared to the environment we just escaped.

"Shoot a few hoops?" Curtis asked.

"Not today. I got a question for you."

"What, man?"

"Could any of your men be involved?"

He thought it over. He lit up another cigarette with his Bic lighter. A bad sign.

"Don't know, man. Don't know."

"Is putting these guys in the grocery store like putting the fox in the henhouse?"

"Know what you mean."

"Hell, I'll chance it. Anything on the Gutman case?"

"Some things I'm startin' to hear, man."

"Like what?"

"Word 'bout our general. Could be a lead."

That was all Curtis would tell me for now. I was pissed off and frustrated but I settled for it.

11

At the office, there was a message to call Johnny D.

"Yeah, Bunco got some complaints," he said. "But no real leads. Seems like there's some white gang out there don't like Vietnamese much. Bunco figures a lot of Vietnamese are just keepin' quiet an' payin' off."

I thought of Curtis and the nervous veterans in the Asian environment of the Tenderloin. Something or someone was being wound up like the rubber band in a kid's model plane. A few more turns and . . . snap!

"Could Vietnam vets be involved?"

"It's possible. But there's no proof."

"Thanks, Johnny."

" 'Thanks, Johnny,' he says. So what's the connection to our knife man? That's how you got me to go to Bunco on this one."

"I'm not sure."

"Bullshit."

"I don't have anything firm. But you'll be the first to know when I do."

"Bullshit once again. I oughta turn you in to Bunco for your scams."

"Are you on duty tonight?"

"No."

"Why don't we cruise around together, then."

"We? We who?"

"You and me," I said.

"I got extra patrols out there. Don't be crazy."

"I'm serious."

"I was gonna take the wife out to a Mexican restaurant."

"Do it tomorrow. She eats Mexican all the time at home, anyway."

"But this way she don't clean up the dishes."

"Gutman is out there poised to strike, for Christ sakes. And you want to go eat a burrito?"

"She'll be pissed." I was getting to him.

"First she's learning English and new she doesn't want to cook. What the hell's the world coming to?"

"All right. All right. But stalking this Gutman guy is like hunting a ghost."

"No shit. He started out in a grave."

"I'll pick you up at dark," Johnny said.

Johnny pulled up in front of the office at seven. We drove around in the unmarked, stripped-down dark green Plymouth that anyone not stoned on drugs would immediately recognize as a police vehicle.

We drove down Van Ness, the spine of the city running through the valley between Pacific Heights on one side and Russian Hill and Nob Hill on the other. It is the widest boulevard in San Francisco with a ninety-three-foot-wide roadway and sixteen-foot-wide sidewalks. Its great width, in fact, served as the firebreak that saved Pacific Heights during the great earthquake and fire of 1906. Once a commercial area and automobile row, it was gradually becoming a residential street with apartments going up all along it.

Johnny kept his police radio on as we cruised its length, passing at various times Harry's Bar, the Hard Rock Cafe, Roselie's, and the Mesquite Bar & Grill. While the once great hangout Henry Africa's was closed now, there was still Tommy's Joynt at Van Ness and Geary, where a beer cost a buck, and Zims, where you got all the coffee refills you wanted for eight-five cents.

"I don't know why I let you talk me into this kinda shit," he complained. "I coulda been eatin' Mexican with my wife an' kids."

"The lure of the chase. The thrill of the hunt. Stop at Taco Bell. My treat."

"Like hell. Take me to the Hard Rock Cafe."

"Not at six bucks a hamburger," I said.

He found a Taco Bell and I sprang for a five-taco special at the drive-up window."

"Too thin," he complained as he scarfed them down.

"Not like your mamma's kielbasa?" I asked.

"Screw you."

Ten minutes later, taco-heavy, we turned off Van Ness at Tommy's Joynt and went around the block to Post to get a one-way street going downtown. At Union Square we made a right and got on Geary, which only ran west. We were driving up Geary Street, past the crowded Kosher delis and the people filling up the sidewalk during the intermission at the American Conservatory Theatre, when we heard the call.

It sounded like Gutman had struck in Polk "Gulch," a four-block strip of Polk Street between Geary and Pine where adult customers openly cruised for teenaged prostitutes—an activity that local merchants said had all the restraint of a shark feed. At the top of the gulch, at the corner of Polk and Pine, twelve-year-olds went for $150. Down at the curbs of Geary, bargain basement tricks went for $20.

We were only a few blocks away. Johnny slashed his way through the traffic and we were at the bottom of the Gulch in less than five minutes.

He pulled the car in behind a station wagon blocking an alley. Two blues were there but no detectives had arrived yet.

"April Fool" was painted in blood above the vehicle.

We looked into the station wagon. The front seat looked like a bucket of red paint had been poured over it. Even though he was covered with blood and his face was distorted in death, I recognized the victim.

"You got an ID?" Johnny asked the blues.

"Nothing on the john. But we're running the license plate," one of them, an overweight middle-aged guy, said.

"Don't bother with that license-plate check," I said.

"You know the guy?" Johnny asked.

"So do you, Johnny. That's our old friend Leo Stubbs."

Leo Stubbs, a sleazeball ex-P.I., almost got me killed last year. We knew his taste in teenaged prostitutes, so I wasn't surprised that he came to his end in the Gulch. Even more appropriate was that he died in the bargain basement section, where tricks were cheap. That was the Leo Stubbs I knew.

"*That* scumbag?" Johnny muttered.

"I guess he got out of jail." I turned away from the sight. He wasn't pleasant to look at. Even worse than when he was alive.

"Must have been a teenybopper hooker with him," Johnny D. said.

"We're gonna start talking to people on the street. But you know how it is. They're gonna be tight assholes," the older cop said.

The other, a younger one with a bushy blond mustache, nodded.

"It's gotta be done," Johnny said. "Find that hooker."

The older cop smirked. Johnny ignored it.

The investigation would continue. Even if nobody gave a damn about a scumbag like Leo Stubbs.

It was time for the last call to Nancy Gutman.

"This is it," I said. "I can't take your money anymore."

"Let me come over so we can talk about it," she said.

I had a feeling that was a bad idea, so naturally I went for it.

It only took Nancy fifteen minutes to get to the office.

"That was quick."

"Light traffic."

I looked out of the front window. Her Mercedes sedan was parked on an angle half on the sidewalk right in front of the building.

"Very creative parking."

"Will I get a ticket?"

I went into my office and came out with a white card with a black cross on it. The card read CLERGY.

"Stick this on your dashboard."

"Would a priest drive a Mercedes?"

"Why not? A Mercedes is like an Oldsmobile these days."

She gave me a funny look but took the card out to the car.

When she came back, she asked, "Don't I need a special license plate?"

"Give me a break, Nancy. I'm all out of clergy plates."

We went into my office and sat down together on the couch. The only light was coming from my desk lamp. I went to switch on the overhead fluorescents.

"Don't put those on," she said. "I hate them."

I didn't put them on. I asked, "Okay? Can I get you anything?"

"Do you have any more of that Stolichnaya Limonaya."

"Yes. But are you sure . . ."

"Don't worry," she interrupted. "I'll just sip it." She took out her pack of Virginia Slims, remembered and put them back in her purse.

I went out to the refrigerator and bar in the hallway and got us half-full pony glasses.

Nancy lifted hers and said, "*Na zdorovye.*"

We clicked glasses as I rejoined her on the couch.

"You're not going to try to find my son before the police do?"

"He's their man. I can't get in the way anymore."

"I see. But what about my granddaughter?"

"I haven't found her but we know she was working in Tahoe."

"As what?"

"As a dealer."

She took out a check from her purse and handed it to me. It went well above what I would have charged her up to now.

"This is more than you owe."

"It's to keep you on the case."

I started to object.

"To find my granddaughter. At least let me have that."

I gave her request serious consideration. I looked at the amount she had written in once again and I looked at the very attractive woman sitting next to me. I made my decision. It wasn't hard.

I nodded, folded up the check, and put it into my wallet. Without guilt. Hell, this was a business with a high overhead.

"But this is just to find Jackie," I said.

"Agreed. Now get me one more vodka. To sip."

I did. With business concluded, I turned my attention to Nancy herself. The suffering of the past weeks hadn't had an effect on her looks. She still appeared a decade younger than her fifties and she still looked well cared for.

She stared back at me. She moved closer to me on the couch and put her hand in mine. I held it in silence for maybe a minute while looking into those enormous eyes.

I let her hand go, got up, and went to the window. When I turned around, she was standing up, ready to leave. I felt that was best for both of us. Her lips brushed mine as we said good night.

Through the window, I saw her stop and light a cigarette in the street. The pinpoint of light disappeared into the front seat of the Mercedes.

She hadn't gotten a ticket.

12

We were into Sunday, the first day of May, and while we were out of the business of hunting Gutman, we still had his daughter to locate. I called Mickey.

"The April Fool Killer got Leo Stubbs," I said.

"Justice works in strange ways."

"How are you doing with the search for Jackie?"

"I think Sherry's starting to come around. I mentioned Jackie's father and that struck a chord. We'll see."

"Does she know that Gutman's the April Fool Killer?"

"No. And I didn't tell her."

"Do you think Gutman will kill again?" she asked.

"April 30 the war ends, but maybe not here." I paused. "You be careful."

"Hey, he only kills white males."

"So far."

"By the way. Was there a dent in the right front fender of the T-Bird?"

"What?"

"Just kidding." She hung up.

I went to the Chew grocery store to talk to Hank and his two younger brothers about the operation. I got all three of them by the cash register behind the deli counter and outlined the plan. "If you don't want the police, these guys in the store are the only way to go."

I explained who the Dragon Seeds were. The brothers, including Hank, were not thrilled but we didn't have a lot of inexpensive options.

"Do you know what a professional bodyguard costs?" I asked.

"No."

"Four hundred dollars a day."

"We cannot accept the Dragon Seeds," the two younger brothers insisted.

"Why not?" I asked.

"Wrong kind of people." The same two brothers, the two who called themselves Reggie and Willie, were adamant.

"Then go to the cops."

"No." On that they all agreed.

"You can trust these men," I insisted and hoped I was right.

"I say yes," Hank announced. He had seniority but they were still skeptical.

"Look. I'll waive my fee if you pay these guys the minimum wage. And you can give them yesterday's bread and salads."

Hank took his brothers off to a corner of the grocery and had a team meeting. When they came back, they were all nodding their heads.

"Okay. Deal, Mr. St. John," Hank said.

We shook hands all around on it.

With that part of the job over, I picked up some bagels, cream cheese, and lox for breakfast. The brothers added some Danishes and put it all on the house.

Hank explained the change of heart. "I explain what waiving fee mean."

At the office, the Chief had left a message on the answering machine that he was nearly done with the juror profiles and that they should be ready this afternoon, which would give the psychologists plenty of time to do their "scientific" interpretations.

There was also a message to call Nancy. I decided to postpone answering.

I wasn't going to waste a beautiful Sunday morning. I worked out in the gym, concentrating on exercises to strengthen my back for the twist serve and on tennis-specific exercises where you do your strokes while holding a ten-pound dumbbell instead of a racket. It's the same theory as the weighted bat for warmup swings in baseball.

But swinging weights is not as much fun as swinging a racket and blasting a tennis ball, so I grabbed my gear and went up to Lafayette park. I picked up a match with a kid from the San Francisco State tennis team. I actually took the first set but then he turned it up a notch. I blew a big lead in the third set and finally lost in a tiebreaker. Despite the loss, I knew I was closer to being ready for Dr. Glenn.

When I got back to the office, Nancy was waiting for me on the porch. All things considered, I wasn't sure I was glad to see her.

"You didn't return my call," she said as she crushed out the cigarette she was smoking.

"I was out all morning. Was it important?"

"No. Not really." She didn't expand on that and I didn't press her.

"Have breakfast yet?" I asked instead.

"No."

"Join me."

As I deprogrammed the alarm on the door, she asked, "Are your partners here?"

"Nope."

"I'd like to meet them."

"I keep them on the road a lot."

Over coffee and bagels, cream cheese, and lox I asked her, "Why did you come over?"

"I don't know. Maybe it's because you're the only person I can talk to about what's happening."

"I think we're making progress on Jackie," I said. "As a matter of fact, one of my partners is in Nevada on the case. Be patient, I hope to have something for you soon."

"I want Vincent stopped."

"So do we all. Have you heard from him?"

"No, I would have told you if I had." She paused. "Are there any further clues?"

"Just that all the victims have recently been to Nevada."

That left her silent. As we ate, a sexual tension grew between us and we both felt uncomfortable. As soon as we finished I started picking up the dishes and Nancy suddenly got up, thanked me for breakfast, and left. This time without any kind of a kiss.

After I cleaned up, I took a nap.

I woke up when I heard the Chief come in. I got dressed quickly and went downstairs. He had the juror profiles.

"Good job."

"Now I am taking a day off. I have a date with a lovely young lady. I have a Seminole jersey ready for her on my boat."

The Chief had a houseboat in Mission Creek. It was a classic bachelor's pad, unlike mine. There was a plush white rug, a metal fireplace, black leather furniture, recessed lighting, and a Chief-sized water bed. On the walls were erotic oriental and Eskimo etchings and prints, mock-racist baseball pennants like the Cleveland Negroes next to real ones like the Atlanta Braves, and a life-size poster of Moses himself in an FSU football uniform. Oriental art pieces, which he claimed were genuine antiques, added a final classy touch.

After he left, I called the messenger service. In fifteen minutes a young uniformed girl with short mouse-brown hair and hazel eyes magnified by oversized glasses arrived on a mountain bicycle and took the juror profiles on their way. I hoped she could make out cars and trucks on the street.

The Chief and I started Monday off with a visit to the Chew grocery stores, where the operation was now in place in the form of Agent Orange eating a popsicle and moving through store aisles that were almost too narrow for him.

I introduced him to the Chief and the two big men eyed each other and shook hands. I could see by the distorted expressions on their faces that they were both giving it their strongest grips.

"You can arm wrestle later," I said when it looked like their handshake was going to last the morning.

"You first," Agent Orange insisted to the Chief.

"Together at the count of three, you both break," I said.

They agreed to that. And on the fourth try, they actually did break.

Agent Orange went back to prowling the aisles and the Chief and I went to talk to Hank.

He told us he had received another threat and that someone was going to be by for a payoff this week. The brothers were glad to have "The Orange," as they called him, with them. I was glad the Orange was there, too.

"How much are they asking for?"

"He did not say."

"What was the threat?"

"Fire."

"Did you say you would pay?"

"He hung up."

After that stop, we took a cable car to Chinatown, where we were to meet Tommy Dong at his new office. The location of it suggested that he had overcome the ancient enmity between the Chinese and the Vietnamese. The actual site of it confirmed that suggestion. It was in a modern architect's office building version of a Chinese pagoda right off Grant Avenue, the broadway of Chinatown.

"He gets on with the Chinese?" I asked.

"Business, Jeremiah. They are the world's biggest gamblers and therefore his best customers."

"Makes sense to me."

Dong's office was on the third level. The red and gold metal door shimmered in waves of light.

Inside, the effect was elegant. The Chief and I stood in a large carpeted reception area that looked like a combination oriental art and gambling museum.

A beautiful Chinese woman with long black hair and velvet-brown eyes rose from a black lacquered desk to greet us.

"Mr. Dong is on the phone," she said. Please have a seat or feel free to look around. My name is Mai, if you have any questions."

Looking around was much more to our taste. I didn't recognize any of the specific objects but I could see that the four main areas of oriental art were represented, bronzes, jade, ceramics, and lacquers. The Chief stopped in front of a bronze vessel in a Plexiglas box sitting on top of a short white pillar. "A ritual bronze from the Zhou dynasty."

I looked around on the pillar for information about the piece. There was none.

"You're making this up, Chief," I said.

He indicated another object. "Bronze Buddha. Sixth century A.D. Give or take a century."

I looked at Mai, who was smiling at the Chief.

"Actually fifth century," she said.

I turned to the Chief.

"I often visit the Asian Art Museum in Golden Gate Park. In a small way I am a collector."

So the art pieces on his houseboat were genuine. "I'm impressed."

"You should be."

There was more to the museum than oriental art. In other Plexiglas boxes were sets of dominolike tiles and pairs of dice.

"Dominoes and dice," I said.

"*Pai gow* and *sic-bo*," the Chief countered. "Now played in Nevada casinos. There is even *pai gow* poker in which two poker hands are played with seven cards. Very big in Tommy's parlors. You should try one of these games."

"Not with you," I said.

"And especially not with Tommy."

"He can see you now," Mai said as she got up from her desk to open his inner office door.

Tommy Dong's office was an extension of the museum in the reception area. Same carpeting and same display cases. With different works of art in a smaller area. There were mainly jade pieces with a few ceramics. The Chief ignored this art and focused on Tommy Dong, who was a piece of work as well. So did I. He looked different than the Tommy Dong I remembered. For one thing, he was now clean shaven. For another, he looked like he had just had a steam facial, a haircut, and a manicure. He also must have dropped twenty pounds. I didn't know exactly how old he was but he looked a lot younger than his years.

And his clothes were different. His body was wrapped in silk. He wore a silk tailored suit in gray-green, a custom-made silk shirt in light green with a TD monogram on the pocket, and a dark green silk tie and matching pocket handkerchief. The man looked smoother than ever. I agreed with the Chief. I wouldn't want to play any games with Tommy.

Tommy stood up behind a black lacquer desk much larger than his receptionist's. The fact that he was tall always surprised me. We shook hands and sat down. The Chief and I were in carved wooden chairs with arms that looked like tiger paws. They had to be authentic antiques; they were uncomfortable enough.

As we were indulging in some ritual small talk, my damn watch alarm went on. I shut it off. I didn't have a car to worry about. At least not in the city.

"I heard from the pricks again," Tommy said. "They're going to burn down one of my parlors if I don't pay off." He picked up a lacquered cigarette box and offered it to us.

We both refused.

"Nobody smokes anymore these days. But we still die."

He shut the box and put it down. "I gave it up myself."

"The places are all covered," the Chief said.

"So let them try," Dong said.

I suggested bringing in the police but he vetoed that idea. I didn't want to dwell on why. I just asked, "Any idea who these guys could be?"

"White men. Americans."

That we knew. "Who don't care much for Vietnamese," I said.

"Or they do not like poker," Chief Moses said.

Tommy gave us a check for services rendered so far.

"Would you care to try to double it in a game of chance?" he asked.

"Like what?" I asked.

The Chief rolled his eyes.

"A dice game. Fish, Shrimp, and Crab."

"No thanks, Tommy," I said. I had heard of that one. A quick way to empty your pockets into the ocean.

"To us, all life is a gamble," Tommy said.

"It's a gamble for us, too. But that doesn't mean I have to lose this check," I said as we turned to leave his office.

In the afternoon I played tennis while the Chief shot baskets in my gym. I came back at three and joined him on the court until he left at three-thirty. I called the Tahoe lodge but there was no answer in Mickey's room.

After finishing off a small sausage pizza I'd had delivered for dinner, I got a call from the Chief.

"The Yellow Suns caught an arsonist at the Oakland parlor. He was setting a fire in the alley behind the building."

"Let's talk to this guy," I said.

"The interrogation has already been carried out by the Yellow Suns. We have the results."

"Fast work."

"Neither we nor Amnesty International would approve of their methods."

"But we accept the results."

"Of course. The mans's name is Christopher Cook. He claims to have been a Vietnam MIA until very recently. He is working for a man who calls himself General Bloodhart."

"That's a start."

"Pain makes a man talkative."

"An old Indian saying?"

The Chief didn't bother to answer.

"Where's Cook now? There are a lot of other questions to ask. Like exactly what is this Bloodhart up to?"

"That is all we have."

"What the hell did the Suns do to him?"

"Unfortunately, the fire department and the police were alerted. That was all the Suns could get from him before the police arrived and arrested him."

"At which point he shut up, of course."

"Of course. And demanded an attorney."

Still the Yellow Suns had done some pretty nice work.

After that conversation, I called Curtis and told him about Bloodhart.

"That's the general," he said.

"Well, I'm getting more on him than you," I complained.

"Hey, man, you're the pro. I'm just an amateur. But I'm tryin'."

"Glad to hear it. Get something, will you?"

"I said I am tryin'."

"Now that we're into May, any possible dates for Gutman to strike?"

"Been thinkin' 'bout it. Only ones I can come up with are the fall of Dien Bien Phu or the capture of *Mayaguez* by the Cambodians. First on May 7. Second on May 12. But I don't know. Seem far-fetched to me. He's been killing on dates that ended the war."

"You've been right so far."

"Yeah, but who knows how a psycho works."

"Bye, Curtis."

I called Dr. Koyota at Letterman. He was surprisingly good na-
tured about our hoax after I told him our real line of work. I could
only assume that Mickey had a lasting effect on the man. He got
back to me in less than an hour and confirmed that there was an
MIA named Christopher Cook missing since 1970.

I considered calling Johnny D. but decided to wait until I had
something more definite. Things were a long way from coming
together yet. Besides, at this point, this was all Bunco to him.

On Tuesday Mickey called me. She had the information on
Jackie Gutman but she wouldn't tell me over the telephone, despite all the empty threats I made. I was annoyed but I couldn't
complain about results. I asked her about the car and she said,
"You'll see." That made me nervous.

I left the Chief in charge of the office and the Chew grocery
case.

Wanting to get up to Tahoe as soon as possible, I called the one-
man Cal-Neva Airlines operation and arranged to be picked up at
the Sausalito base at two o'clock. The Chief drove me over the
Golden Gate Bridge, complaining about the traffic that was already
building up to standard Bay Area gridlock.

This time the plane was full of typical-looking commuters. The
flight was flawless and I was at the lodge before three-thirty.

I got a key to the apartment and let myself in. There was a note
from Mickey. She was out on the tennis courts with the club pro. I
got into my tennis clothes.

Before I went out to the courts, I checked on my car in the
parking lot. It was just as I had left it. Perfect.

13

"So that's what she's been doing," I said as I propped my racket up against the net. "Working at what's euphemistically known as a ranch."

"Yes," Mickey said as she took the sweatbands off her wrists.

"How did you get Sherry to talk?"

"I convinced her I knew a rich relative who was interested in finding Jackie."

"Which is true. What about Gutman? Did Sherry talk to him."

"Oh, yeah. His methods were less subtle than ours. He went right to force and pain and got his information."

With this case less urgent than the search for Gutman, I said, "Let's get off the court and rent a boat. I'll go see Jackie tomorrow."

We rented a small two-seater powerboat and cruised across the northwest corner of the lake into King's Beach, where we saw a drug sale go down right in front of us as we tied up the boat by the city clubhouse. We paid a guest fee and used the weight room and the glass-enclosed hot tub, which was large enough for a mid-sized Roman orgy. Kids were diving into it like it was a swimming pool. In a sand pit behind us a professional beach volleyball tournament was in full and hot progress.

"Some hunks," Mickey noted of the young and blond Southern

California beachboy types playing the game tanned and shirtless.

"What about me?"

"I'm talking serious hunks here, Jeremiah."

"So I'm not a serious hunk. But can those muscle-bound guys play tennis?"

"Can you?"

I got out of the tub, went down to the lake, and dove into the freezing water. It was a shock to the system.

Mickey followed me out but didn't dive into the lake. Smart woman. We untied the boat and cruised back to Incline.

"Nice ride," Mickey said as we skimmed over water so clear that rocks fifty feet beneath us looked like they could tear out the bottom of our boat. Then she grinned. "Did you check out your precious car?"

"First thing I did was go to the parking lot. Thanks for taking care of it. How was driving it?"

"Like driving a pickup truck."

"That's how it's supposed to be. It puts you in contact with the road."

"That's okay for a boat on water. It's not what I want from a car on asphalt."

We dropped the boat off in Incline and I collected my deposit.

We spent the early evening playing doubles with the same couple from last week. This time we beat them easily.

"You really are improving," Mickey said.

"I know. My muscles remember what to do."

We showered, I built a fire, and Mickey, who had stocked up on food, cooked some pasta which we had with a bottle of Chianti. After dinner, something was clicking between us again. We both felt it.

But the first and only move belonged to Mickey, who said, "I'm exhausted. I'm going to sleep."

Which left me alone in the living room with television and a dying fire. I watched a made-for-TV movie about a Miami private eye who worked with his son and daughter. I was glad to see that they gave him a harder time than even my partners gave me. Unfortunately, I dozed off and missed the solution to the mystery. Just like life at the agency.

Mickey was still asleep when I left the next morning. I figured it would take me about an hour and a half to get to my destination, some twenty miles from Reno.

I was right. I arrived in the middle of the morning, which I hoped would be a slow time.

There was no problem finding the place. The big sign on the main building read Seven Veils Ranch. As I had pointed out to Mickey, not a good omen for someone with my name. Next to that structure were two smaller stucco buildings that looked like crosses between motels and shopping malls.

Jackie Gutman had progressed from runaway to blackjack dealer to prostitute in one of the largest of Nevada's thirty-six legal brothels.

Mickey had played her part to get the information and now it was my turn to play the john (minus the St.). I hoped Jackie still resembled her high school photo.

The Seven Veils Ranch had everything you'd ever need in the middle of the desert. There was a cafeteria, a full-scale hairdressing salon, a small library, a health clinic, a movie theater, and a game room that looked like a boardwalk arcade. All of these had signs that read: FOR EMPLOYEES AND INDEPENDENT CONTRACTORS ONLY. I wondered what an independent contractor was.

I went into the main building and was greeted by a Hostess with an elaborately frosted beehive hairdo dressed in a black evening gown. I knew she was a Hostess because that's what the sign said on her desk. In a corner of the small entrance room there was a very plain woman in a mannish suit sitting in a teller's cage with the sign CASHIER hanging over it. So I knew she was the Cashier. But I didn't know much else. What was I supposed to do? Do I offer to pay now? Is there a *prix fixe*?

"Hello. May I be of assistance?" the Hostess asked. "Would you like to meet one of our girls?"

"Yes." I didn't expect any of the women would be using their real names so there wouldn't be any point in asking for Jackie Gutman.

The Hostess explained that I could meet a girl through the traditional lineup in the parlor. If I found one that suited me, I could then take her to the Seven Veils Bar for a drink. If things worked out, we could then repair to the lady's bedroom.

She got specific. "House rules prohibit any discussion in the bar area between the lady and client of proposed sexual activities. When you go with the lady to her room, those matters are discussed and a price is agreed upon. The house does not set the price. Our ladies are independent contractors who rent their rooms from us and share their earnings with us."

Now I knew what an independent contractor was.

She continued, moving into a set speech undoubtedly prepared for all Hostesses by the Nevada Division of Tourism in Carson City. "While sexual activity brings with it the threat of sexual disease, no prostitute in a legal Nevada brothel has tested positive for AIDS. We believe the controlled environment we have diminishes the risks of sexual disease. Of course our women, according to state law, must have monthly tests for AIDS and weekly exams for other sexually transmitted diseases. In addition, it is the house policy that condoms must be worn for all sexual activities. I hope you have no objection because there are no exceptions. The Seven Veils provides sex at its safest."

"I'm surprised you don't have a seal of approval from the Surgeon General hanging over the door instead of a horseshoe."

"If he was honest about it, we'd get one." She smiled.

I smiled back at her. We were having a fun time. I had the etiquette down. Now it had to bring me Jackie. I went for the parlor lineup.

She hit a series of buttons that I assumed alerted all of the women in rooms that were not in use.

The parlor we stepped into ten minutes later had red flocked wallpaper covered with elaborately framed pictures of naked cherubim floating about on clouds, looking chubby and cute. The floor was thickly carpeted with a gold rug that matched the color of the frames. Overall it looked like a Western whorehouse should.

I stood with the Hostess in front of a line of nine women. They all wore long red gowns with tops that looked like slip tops and backless gold shoes. Hair color ranged from platinum to blue-black, skin color from ebony to pink, and heights from five to six feet. Most of them had decent figures but two of them were just a little chubby, like the cherubim.

I inspected them closely. I felt embarrassed and ridiculous. I couldn't tell how they felt. Their faces were blank. There was no Jackie.

"How could I meet some others?" I whispered to my Hostess.

My Hostess looked annoyed. She sighed. "You can go to the bar. When a woman is available, she will come down there. You can initiate an introduction with any woman who is alone."

"I'll try that." I escaped the pissed-off stares of the nine independent contractors by heading for the bar.

It was a basic operation. A few dozen bottles and one bartender behind a wooden bar no more than six feet long. There were no barstools in front of it. You had to sit at tables for two spread around the dimly lit room. The lighting was obviously set to assist the older independent contractors.

I ordered a tequila sunrise from a cocktail waitress who wore a button that said DRINKS ONLY. I proceeded to nurse it for the next hour. There were two other men, in three-piece suits, sitting alone at tables in the bar. Several women came into the bar and talked to the bartender so we could get a good look at them. None looked like Jackie. After a while the two men both left with women. Gradually they were replaced by three other men. These looked different. Like tired truck drivers taking a break. They were dressed in plaid shirts, down vests, and baseball hats. More women came. More men left with them.

The woman who came in about noon looked like a hardened, heavily made-up, version of the Jackie whose picture I had memorized. Her red hair was now a wild curly tangle instead of straight but I was sure it was her.

She moved with grace into the bar, dressed in a short slip trimmed with lace and held up with spaghetti straps. Her figure was better than any I had seen in the lineup. I went up to her before any of the truck drivers still in the bar could make a move and brought her back to my table.

Following the rules of the place, we exchanged names. I gave her my real one and she gave me, as I expected, her professional one: Jackie Grant. Close enough. According to the house etiquette, I couldn't bring up sex at the bar. It probably wasn't a good idea to discuss Vincent Gutman, either. So I talked about the desert weather while she ordered a vodka on the rocks.

She looked bored as hell as she sipped her drink, which was probably more water than vodka.

I got to the point. "Can we go to your room?"

"That's what I'm here for," she said with a forced smile.

I paid the hefty tab and we left the bar. Her room was in the building that contained the mall shops. It looked like the kind of room you got when you had to stay in one of those low-rate chain motels that stand like concrete forts along our California highways. The furniture was plastic, the carpeting was ancient orange shag, and the place smelled of bug spray and disinfectant. There was a king-size bed that was a cut above the rest of the furniture. There was no phone but Jackie had apparently brought in her own portable TV. The window looked out on the parking lot.

She asked, "What'll it be?" as she flopped down on the bed. Hardly a seductive pose.

"What do you charge for a half hour of talk?" I sat in an uncomfortable chair by a small wooden desk that didn't go with the rest of the decor. Like the TV, it must be her own, I thought.

"You some kinda weirdo. Look, I gotta log in with the cashier downstairs. And I gotta log in what the customer is buying."

"You keep records like that?"

"Sure. It gives us standards for setting rates for... Well, you know."

"What's a straight lay go for?"

"Dressed or undressed?"

"You or me?"

"Me, dummy." She laughed. "You gotta get undressed."

"Why?"

She handed me a plastic card with some more house rules. Customers had be examined first for signs of drug use or herpes or other disease. The Hostess had not mentioned this requirement.

"Look. Nobody takes their clothes off. Log in whatever you want. We'll just talk," I said.

She sighed wearily. "Okay. I'll call it oral sex." She had a sense of humor.

"A hundred dollars for the half hour. And I'll have to set that timer." She pointed to a digital alarm clock by the bed. Better than an hourglass.

"Fine." I didn't mention this one was on her grandmother. "You take credit cards?"

"Yeah. American Express. We've just been added." I handed her my card. She looked at it and said, "I need your license."

"Why?"

"For an ID check."

I showed her three more credit cards.

"I need to see your license."

"Why?"

"To get your address."

"What for?"

"In case there's a recall." She was annoyed with me.

"A recall?"

In exasperation she said, "In case we have to trace down our sexual partners because of a transmitted disease. Okay?"

"But we're not having sex."

"It's the rule. I gotta bring your license and credit card to the cashier." She got up from the bed.

"Bet married men don't appreciate this routine."

"If that's your problem, we promise to be discreet. Our business depends upon it."

"I bet," I said, nodding, letting her think I was married and worried.

She disappeared with my credit card and my license. Time to check out the room. I went right to the desk. The middle drawer was locked. I pulled out a narrow plastic case in which I have a number of metal sticks of various sizes and shapes but all with a circumference of no more than one sixteenth of an inch. I didn't usually carry around lock picks. If the cops picked you up and they were in your possession, you were in it deep. But I thought I might need them today. Besides, I left my S&W at the lodge. I needed something to make me feel like a private detective.

I tried several sticks until the lock turned. When I opened the drawer, I found it full of cash, unreported tips, as I had expected. But there was also a notebook. As far as I could tell, it contained the names of Jackie's customers, complete with addresses and sexual activities purchased. When I found all of Gutman's victims listed, including Leo Stubbs I knew what I had. I also knew my name was going to join the customer list.

She opened the door and was startled to see the book in my hands. She didn't look bored anymore.

"What the fuck are you doing?" she shouted as she slammed the door behind her.

I held up the notebook. "This is what we're going to talk about."

"Fuck you!" She started back for the door but I grabbed her before she could get away.

Trapped in the room, she was trying to reach a button near the bed. An alarm if a customer got out of hand.

"Stop fighting me. I just need some information. And maybe I can help you." I was holding both of her wrists.

"Help me? What are you talking about?"

"Give me a chance to explain."

"No."

"Stop fighting." I increased the pressure on her wrists.

"Ow. Ow. Please!" She stopped struggling. I let her go and she sat down on the bed. "Who are you?" she asked.

"You know my name. And I know yours. It's Jackie Gutman."

"So? No woman uses her real name here."

"So your father, who everyone thought was dead in Vietnam, came to see you."

"So?"

"So he got a copy of these names."

"Maybe."

"Do you know what he's been doing?"

"What're you talking about?"

"You don't, do you?"

"I said I don't know what you're talking about."

"He's killing these men." I waved the notebook over her.

"That's crazy."

"Have you heard of the April Fool Killer?"

"Yeah. Vaguely. On the TV news."

I said, "Well, that's your father. And his victims are all your former customers."

She looked genuinely stunned. She started shaking her head violently. "Oh, God. No. No. No!"

"He was up here, wasn't he?" I sat next to her on the bed and put my arm around her bare shoulders. Her skin had become clammy. She was sobbing. I repeated the question. "He was up here?"

"Yes." I could barely hear her for the sobbing.

"He got the names from your notebook?"

"Yes. I had another copy."

I took my arm from her shoulders. She shuddered.

"What did he do when he found you?"

"He hit me. I was scared. He was raging around. Tossing the room. I thought he was going to kill me. I ran out of the room and hid in another girl's. When I came back, he was gone."

"With your list of customers and their sexual preferences. He had some business to take care of."

"Oh, God!" She covered her face with her hands.

I tried some good news. "Your grandmother's looking for you."

"So?"

"She's a woman with money."

"What's that to me?"

"You're her only grandchild."

She looked up. Most of the heavy makeup had washed off. She looked better. "Please. Don't tell her about me. Don't tell her what I'm doing."

"She can help you."

"Please."

I made no promises. "She hired me."

"I'm getting out of the business. I'm expecting to come into some money myself."

"Oh? How?"

"An old customer...a sick, lonely old man. A very sick man. "He's...leaving me some money."

I held up the notebook. "Seems to me it must be against house rules for you to be keeping a separate log like this. What do you do? Memorize the names and addresses when you go to the cashier? Then write them in when the customer leaves? Along with what they paid for? This could make the management here very suspicious." I stood up.

"What do you want with those names?"

"What do *you* want with them?" I asked, avoiding using the word blackmail.

She didn't answer.

"I want the police to warn these men. Like a recall. You know."

She thought it over. "I can't let you do that. The police will want to know where the names came from."

"You didn't do anything illegal."

"I can't let you take it."

"You don't have much choice."

She slipped a small revolver out from under the mattress. I was getting sloppy.

"Give it to me," she said.

So I did. I chopped her right arm with the edge of the notebook and then grabbed her wrist. The gun fell to the floor.

"You won't get out of here with it," she said.

"We'll see." First I ripped out the wire that led to the button by the bed. Then I opened her closet and took the belt of a robe and tied her to the bedpost. She started cursing and screaming and I had to gag her with a silk scarf.

I patted her on the shoulder and said, "Hey, don't write off your grandmother. She's a great lady." When she started to struggle with the knotted belt, I added, "I'll send this anonymously to the cops. They won't know where I got it."

I left with the notebook. I kept my promise to Jackie by stopping at an office supply store in Reno and trying out a typewriter. Just enough to type an anonymous note. At the post office I convinced a nice old woman that I had a sprained wrist and she addressed an Express Mail envelope for me. I sent the notebook and the note to Johnny D. Untraceable.

Mickey and I had our last meal in Nevada at a romantic place called The Pier, in Incline. We had a table by the window and we watched the lake darken as the sun set. From the South Shore, the casinos burst into pillars of light against the black mountains. Smaller points of light rimmed the lake in an unbroken chain.

Mickey ordered roast duck in orange sauce and I ordered the duck in green peppercorn sauce. We had a perfect bottle of Sonoma Gewurztraminer to go with the meal.

After dinner we drove to the Silver Bar Casino. Mickey went to a roulette wheel and I found Opal at a No Smoking blackjack table. She acted like I was a stranger. Maybe she was angry with me for not calling her. I didn't care. In a half hour I won back the cost of the meal and quit while I was ahead.

In our rooms, Mickey and I kissed as we had in the past, like we meant it.

"I don't know," Mickey said.

"I do."

"You always do."

"Why not?" I asked.

"I don't know what I'm feeling. I don't want to go to bed with you and wake up upset about it the next morning."

"Then I won't let you fall asleep."

It wasn't working . She untangled herself from me and stood up. "Beat Glenn at tennis," she said.

"What?"

"You heard me," she said as she disappeared into her room.

I knew she was just putting me off but I wasn't going to let her forget her challenge. I was ready to turn it into some kind of medieval fantasy where I had a task to perform to win the lady.

I slept fitfully, dreaming of a sword battle with Dr. Earnhard and then slaying a fire-breathing dragon in a dark cave. Only my sword kept turning into a tennis racket with broken strings.

14

We got up early Thursday morning for the drive back. After using the seaplane commute, I was spoiled. The car ride took over four times as long. It didn't bother Mickey, who slept most of the way.

When we got back to Octavia Street, the Chief was at his desk talking on the phone to his stockbroker. *The Wall Street Journal* was open in front of him.

"Welcome back. I have a hot tip," he said as he covered the mouthpiece.

"On what?" Mickey asked.

"Oil. Indians love oil. A thousand shares at that price," he told the broker and hung up. "The company is rumored to be a take-over target."

"Is this insider trading?" I asked.

"Do not look a tip horse in the mouth."

"Anything new on the threats to Dong and the Chew brothers?" I asked.

"No. We just wait."

"What about this General Bloodhart?" I asked.

"No. But next time we will not lose our man to the police. The next extortionist we catch will lead us to this general."

"Let's hope so. How's our business going otherwise?" I asked.

"We have a new client. A man who has a condom-vending oper-

119

ation. Someone is vandalizing the machines in gay bars."

"Should make for some unusual stakeouts," I said.

"This is one for the camcorder," the Chief said.

"We found Jackie Gutman working in a legal brothel outside of Reno," I said. I went on to fill in the Chief on the names in her notebook.

"The April Fool Killer has made no more threats," the Chief said.

Gutman was the big loose end I hoped the police would tie up soon.

"We're letting the police look for him," I said.

"Good," Mickey and Chief Moses agreed.

"Now for the Condom Vandal." The Chief got out the camcorder and left to install it in the men's room of a likely gay bar in the Castro.

While Mickey and I were settling back into the office, the phone rang. It was Hank Chew at the grocery store with what we had been waiting for. The man to lead us to Bloodhart.

"Must hurry. We are holding the bad man."

"Don't call the police," I said. "We're on our way."

Mickey and I sprinted to the grocery. I beat her there by about twenty-five yards. As I always told her, it was those high heels that slowed her down. We both arrived out of breath.

There had been no need to hurry. Agent Orange had everything under control. He had stuffed the bad man into a crate and was sitting on top of the box. All the brothers were standing by.

The man in the box was pounding violently on its insides and screaming to get out.

"Let him out," I said.

Agent Orange stood up. The top of the crate flew open and a thin guy with a heavy beard, dressed in army camouflage fatigues, popped out like a jack-in-the-box.

"You shits! You shits!" he yelled at us. He was shaking; tears were streaming down his cheeks. He looked at us, then at Agent Orange. "That's how the fuckin' VC kept me prisoner. In a cage no bigger than that box. I was goin' crazy."

"Sorry, man. I didn't know. You okay?" Agent Orange asked.

"Yeah, I'm okay." He looked at Mickey and me. "You cops?"

"No. Private investigators protecting our friends here from your sleazy racket."

"These gooks?" He gestured toward the Chew brothers.

"Yes. These Vietnamese," Mickey said.

"Fuck 'em all."

"We'd like to ask you some questions," I said.

"And fuck you, too."

"He ask for two thousand dollar. We got no two thousand dollar, Mr. St. John," Hank said. I didn't necessarily appreciate my name getting announced in front of our extortionist but it was too late to do anything about it now. "He say we pay him or the grocery burn down."

"You going to talk to us?" I asked the man.

"You got a cigarette?"

Agent Orange shook out a Camel for him. The guy lit it with the last match in his pack. He threw the empty pack to the floor. When he turned away, I picked it up and saw that it had the name of a bar in Mendocino County on it.

"How 'bout a bottle a beer?" he asked, looking at the cooler at the back of the store.

"How about a name?"

"Dick."

Mickey got him a bottle of Henry's. Love that lady.

"Dick what?" I was dumb enough to ask.

"Suckmine."

"Look, asshole. We don't have to be polite about this."

I grabbed him by the shirt and pushed him back against a wall. Some beer spilled on his fatigues.

"Fuck you!" he shouted.

"You're getting me pissed off," I said. "Are you going to answer some questions or do we put you back in the box until you're ready."

He looked panicked.

"Let's talk," I said.

"Not the box," he shouted as he made a break for the door. I tackled him around the knees and he went down. But he managed to hold on to the beer and the cigarette.

"You talk. Or you get the box."

"All right. All right. Whaddya wanna know?"

"That's better." I let him get up.

"Christ," he said as he puffed on the Camel and switched to the beer.

Agent Orange moved closer to him. He looked almost protective of the man.

"Do you target Vietnamese operations?" I asked.

He took another puff. "Fuckin' gooks. These guys were gettin' fat as hogs in Saigon while me an' my buddies were gettin' our asses shot off for 'em." He crushed his cigarette out on the floor.

"I don't want to debate the Vietnam War. I just want some goddamn answers," I said.

"So ask."

"Who's running your racket?" I asked.

"Ask another."

"Are you the guys trying to extort money from Tommy Dong?"

"That fuckin' gook. No."

"Bullshit," I said. "You're working for General Bloodhart."

That seemed to have some effect. The guy's face went pale.

"I gotta take a leak," the man said as he put the beer bottle down.

"Tough," I said,

"Look," he begged, "I don't wanna wet my pants. I got a thing about bein' in a box—"

Before I could say anything, Agent Orange offered, "I'll take him to the john."

We let him take "Dick."

Which turned out to be a big mistake. Agent Orange came back alone.

"Where the hell's our man?" I yelled.

"He got away. There was a back door and he made a break for it."

Agent Orange was at least twice the size of our man. "Shit," I said. I ran into the street but he was nowhere to be seen. I ran down the alley to the back door. No sign of him. "Dick" had escaped.

In the store, I said to Agent Orange, "I know he was a vet. I know you were feeling for him—"

"He was in the Air Cavalry—same as me," Agent Orange explained. "You heard him say this was like when he was captured by the Viet Cong. He started to crack up in there. It wasn't no act."

"So you let him go."

"He got away. I told you."

"But you didn't try to stop him," Mickey said.

Agent Orange shrugged.

"Did he tell you anything else?" I asked. Maybe we could still salvage something from this fiasco.

"Yeah. He said Bloodhart would napalm our asses if we didn't back off."

"Let's get something straight. You pull this kind of shit once more and we never use the Dragon Seeds again. Understand? You will blow it for your brothers. Understand?"

"Screw you."

"We needed some information."

"And now you got the Bloodhart name. Just like you wanted. So what's the damn problem?"

"I wanted to find out more. Like whether this guy was another of our MIA's."

"He seemed like it."

"That's not enough. I wanted his real name. And I wanted to ask him about Mendocino County. We need a lead to get at Bloodhart." I held up the pack of matches.

"Okay," Agent Orange said. "The guy got to me. I won't screw up again, I swear."

"You think he come back?" Hank asked.

"I don't know. But I imagine you'll hear from them again. It looks bad for the protection racket when somebody beats them at their game."

He nodded his head several times.

"We're going to need someone to stay in the store tonight. I take that arson threat seriously," I said.

"I'll take it tonight. On the house," Agent Orange said.

"You got it," Hank said.

"That's not all we have," Mickey said. She took a plastic bag from the deli counter and wrapped up the beer bottle. "You wanted an ID, Jeremiah. Let's get these prints lifted."

"Brilliant," I said to Mickey.

"Thanks," Agent Orange said to her. "That saves my ass some." Mickey smiled at us both.

We drove to Letterman with the bottle. After a few smiles from Mickey, Dr. Koyota agreed to send it to a lab for a fingerprint check.

When he called us later that afternoon, he confirmed that the fingerprints belonged to another MIA, a Richard Martini.

"Martini, Cook, and Gutman. We have a pattern," I said.

"But no lead on the general," Mickey said.

"How are we going to explain to the Chief that we lost our man?"

"We, Jeremiah?"

I laughed. "If the Yellow Suns can lose Cook to the cops, I guess we can lose Martini to Agent Orange."

"This general is as hard to get a line on as Gutman."

"Another spook," I said.

Nancy called that afternoon about her granddaughter.

"We found Jackie."

"You have? Wonderful. God . . . to have something good come out of all this. How is she?"

"Well . . ." I hedged. It would all come out in the newspapers anyway. And this way it would make some sense of her son's rampage. I said, "That depends on how you look at it. She's a prostitute in one of Nevada's largest legal brothels."

"Oh, no, Jeremiah."

I waited.

"Are you sure it was her?"

"Absolutely. I'm sorry."

"What happened to her? How did she end up in a place like that?" She was asking herself more than she was asking me.

"I know what happened to your son. He found her there and got hold of her list of customers. That's who he's been killing."

She took a deep breath. "Does she know?"

"Now she does."

"What about the police?"

"They've got the list of names. All the men are being warned."

"Do you think it's over?" she asked.

"Vincent hasn't made any more threats," I said.

"How can I reach Jackie?"

I gave her the number of the ranch. "She goes by Jackie Grant." I added, "She said she was quitting."

"That's what they all say, isn't it?"

"Don't be too hard on her."

"I won't be. She is my flesh and blood and that's all that matters. I can help her. Is she on drugs?"

"No. This is a clean operation. You should see it. A clinic, a shopping mall, movies, you name it. A kind of Disneyland whorehouse."

She hesitated. "Thanks, Jeremiah. For everything."

She hung up. I could concentrate on the tennis double date I had with Mickey, Dr. Earnhard, and one of his ex-wives tonight. Mickey had finally called the doctor from Tahoe on Wednesday and set it up for tonight. It was the introduction I wanted.

It turned out to be an interesting mixed doubles match. The doctor, who asked me to call him Glenn, looked as handsome in person as he looked on TV, except that I was just about certain he was wearing a toupee. I teamed up with his ex-wife Gloria, who was blond, well put together, and quite good with a racket. We managed to beat Mickey and Glenn in three sets. Gloria, I had to admit, was the main reason for our victory. Glenn asked me for a singles match. We settled on a date nearly two weeks away. Enough time for me to smooth the rough edges off my game.

"You're a tough man to pin down," he said.

"It's that crazy P.I. schedule."

On the way back to the clubhouse, I grinned at Mickey and said, "You're enjoying this."

"You know what? I am," she whispered.

In the bar over drinks, I noticed again what an attractive woman Mrs. Ex was. I also noticed that for an ex-wife, she got on awfully well with the doctor.

15

Friday morning, May 6. No April Fool threats in the morning paper. Maybe the rampage was over. The answering machine told me that Johnny wanted to talk to me. I assumed he wanted to ask me some questions about the list of brothel customers that had been sent to him. I wasn't in any mood to be interrogated. So I went to the tennis courts.

At Lafayette Park, I ran into the same San Francisco State tennis player and we got in two hard sets. The kid was raising my game to a new level. Getting me ready for Glenn.

At the office, except for what we were calling the Great Condom Caper Case, we could concentrate on the hunt for Bloodhart.

"I am not impressed," the Chief said when I explained how Martini had escaped from us at the grocery store. "We have no trail to follow to Bloodhart."

"I know."

"How many more of these men do we have to catch?" he asked.

"What about Curtis?" Mickey asked.

"I'll check on it," I volunteered. I was getting more and more annoyed with Curtis. I called him and said, "Damn, you should have come up with something by now on this Bloodhart."

"You come up with anythin', man?"

"No. Not a way to get at him."

"So don't you be talkin'. I stay on it." Curtis hung up.

We divided up the cases. The Chief left to check on the camcorder setup in the gay bar. Mickey and I left to visit Dong's local poker parlors. The Yellow Suns had everything under control. We decided to inspect the one in Sonoma. The weather was great for a drive into wine country. We checked on the stakeout there. The Yellow Suns had that one as covered as all the others. Everything was quiet. So quiet that we played a few hands of Seven Card Stud in the Sonoma parlor while hoping one of Bloodhart's men would show up.

The players were mostly retired men, with a few elderly women who looked like they were killing time until they could get to their church bingo game. People with time on their hands. The kind of people who usually wound up on juries for the big cases just because of that. The game was slow and friendly and the stakes never got very high—helped out by a house limit. The house took its cut and the dealer kept everybody honest. And no one hit the parlor.

Back in the city, we stopped at the Chew grocery store, where Agent Orange was on duty. No problems to report. Except for the brother Reggie who complained, "These Dragon Seeds eat like hell."

"You're paying minimum wage," I reminded him.

He covered his ears and shook his head but didn't say anything else. I took it as a Vietnamese gesture of acceptance.

The Chief was at the office. I told him about our tour of the Tommy Dong empire.

He told us about his problems with the Condom Vandal. "Three more vending machines have been hit. I am trying a new bar."

"Just make sure nobody rips off the video equipment," I said.

"It is behind a vent for the heating system in the men's room."

"And if you get a picture of the guy?" Mickey asked.

"Someone will know him."

"I don't think he's leaving his name and address on the wall in these johns," I said.

"If I get him on tape, the Great Tracker will find him."

"You're into this case," I said.

"Condoms save lives."

"They could use you as a host at the Seven Veils Ranch," I said.

Chief Moses grinned. "I almost forgot. Johnny D. has been trying to reach you."

"Any message?" I asked.

"He said your ass is in a sling."

"So what's new," Mickey noted.

I looked out the front window. No police car. Yet. "Let's get out of here and get some dinner." We went to a new Mexican restaurant in our square mile of the city. The place was done in beige adobe, red clay tile, straw matting, and south of the border posters. The food was resort Mexican, which meant a lot of mesquite-grilled dishes. The grilled swordfish was perfect.

"Keep that one on your list," the Chief said to Mickey as we left the place.

The Chief drove Mickey home and I went back to the Victorian. I got a snifter of Courvoisier and one of my favorite Travis McGee novels. The answering machine had Johnny D.'s messages, which I erased. The police could hunt down Gutman now. Gutman had made no more threats. And I had to believe Jackie's customers had been warned.

Halfway through chapter three, I saw Johnny D.'s unmarked car pull up and parallel park in front of our building. I went downstairs and let him in before he could start pounding on the door and shout, "Open up. Police."

"I've been trying to get in touch with you, Jeremiah," he said as we went up the stairs.

"I've been out of town." I said as I handed him a beer and we sat down at the kitchen table.

"I know you sent me that list of names."

"What list?"

"Cut the bull."

"I have clients to protect." Although Jackie herself was hardly much of a client.

"Cooperate. We're trying to save some lives."

"So am I. Maybe not the same ones."

"You thought you were so smart. Nothing in your handwriting. But we pulled your fingerprints from the note you typed."

"Bullshit." I had held it with a Kleenex.

"Will you just talk, Jeremiah?"

"All off the record. Cannot be used against me—all that stuff."

"This is a conversation between friends. I'm off duty. To prove it, I'll have another beer."

I gave him another Henry's and poured some more Courvoisier into my snifter. Johnny just looked at it.

"We were able to alert most of the men on it. The married ones weren't too happy about the call but we were discreet. We didn't leave messages with wives or girlfriends. But why was Gutman targetin' these guys?"

"He doesn't like johns."

"Cut the crap. You gave me a list of customers at a Nevada whorehouse. What whorehouse and why's he hittin' them?"

"He hasn't made another threat, has he?"

"No. Just another victim. This time a woman who worked at one of those legal brothels."

"What?" I coughed up some cognac.

"That's why I need the name of the place where you got that list of johns. There may be a connection."

"It was the Seven Veils Ranch," I said.

"That's it. Bad luck for somebody with your name."

I started up from the table. "Maybe." There was a sinking feeling in my gut. "You have a name?"

"Yeah. But the Nevada cops figure it's a phoney. Called herself Jackie Grant."

That hit me hard. It was bad luck or worse. But I pushed on. "How'd they know it was Gutman?"

"The MO. She was found stabbed to death in the desert about a mile from the ranch. April Fool was painted in blood on some rocks."

"What was she doing out there?" I sat back down.

"The Reno cops figure she was meeting somebody. It was some kinda vista point. With a parkin' area."

"How'd she get out there?"

"A woman gave her a ride."

"One of the prostitutes?"

"Apparently not. It was a broad in an old red Corvette."

I started to ask another question when Johnny interrupted me.

"You're doin' all the damn askin'. I got some questions. What's the connection between Gutman and this whorehouse?"

"I'll make it real simple. Jackie Grant's real name is Jackie Gutman. She was Vincent's daughter. The men on the list were her customers. Vincent Gutman's been wiping them out one by one."

"Christ. So that's what sent him off the deep end."

"Guys have killed for a lot less."

"You should have sent me the name of the whorehouse, Jeremiah."

"And she might still be alive."

"Yeah. We woulda picked her up."

"I promised her that wouldn't happen." I took a deep breath. "Goddamn!" I slammed my fist down on the table.

"I'm sorry, Jeremiah."

I felt ill.

After Johnny left, I called Nancy to make sure she was home.

"Something's wrong, isn't it?" she asked. "I can tell."

"Wait till I get to your place." I checked the Nob Hill address and drove to Nancy's condo. It was on the top story of the building and had a great view of the sparkling magic carpet of the city below. The furniture was French Provincial and the Picasso and Dali paintings on the walls were original.

"Your granddaughter's been murdered," I said as we sat together on a silky couch in front of the marble fireplace. I didn't know how else to say it.

She put her head into her hands. "Do they know who did it?"

"The police believe Vincent did it."

"I don't believe it."

"It makes sense. You hit the johns, sure, but then you go to the source."

She raised her head. "He wouldn't kill his own daughter. No matter what."

"You haven't seen him in sixteen years."

"I still know him."

This wasn't the time to argue.

"Stay on the case, Jeremiah. I know he didn't do this."

"Look, he killed five men. He's not in his right mind."

"Not his own daughter."

"He saw her as a whore!"

"He still wouldn't do it. No matter what she was."

"You can't know that."

"A mother knows."

For her sake, I wanted to believe her. "Okay, I'll try to prove he was innocent in one out of six murders."

We drank a vodka and I left her to her new sorrow. I went back to the Victorian and called Mickey. "What kind of car did Sherry Wine drive?" I asked her.

"An old red Corvette. Just the kind of piece of junk you'd like. What's this about?"

I told her. Then I called the Chief and told him my plans with Mickey for tomorrow.

Saturday morning Mickey and I were in the seaplane heading to Tahoe and the Silver Bar Casino.

"Beats driving," she said.

"Some people commute like this."

"What do they do for a living?"

"Don't ask. I met some of them."

This time we were alone with the pilot. It was costing us four hundred dollars but it was worth it. I wanted to get to Sherry Wine before anyone else did.

The seaplane dropped us off at the dock behind the casino. I got a Reno newspaper from a dispenser and found the Jackie Grant story inside on page five. We went in. Sherry Wine was in the nightclub area rehearsing.

Joe Coglin was there, too, looking and acting as charming as ever.

"When can we expect that TV show to be on?" he asked with a leer.

"Next month. After the editing," Mickey said, playing it straight.

"Could you give the girls a break?" I asked. "I need to talk to Sherry."

Joe scowled but gave the women a ten-minute break.

We went over to Sherry, who was perspiring heavily. She grabbed a towel and her sweatshirt and tried to dry off. Mickey introduced me as a private detective friend looking into Jackie's death.

"Into what?" she asked. "Jackie's death? I don't believe it. I was just with her."

"Jackie was murdered out at the point. The police believe the April Fool Killer did it," Mickey explained.

"That San Francisco nut?"

"That's him," I said.

"Come off it." She looked at Mickey. "I didn't see it on TV."

"It's true, Sherry. Jackie Gutman was murdered yesterday," Mickey said.

I handed her the newspaper opened to the story. She read it slowly. Maybe she read it twice because it took her a long time to finish. Finally she said, "God. The April Fool Killer? Why would he murder her?"

"Because he's her father," I said.

"God. That's insane."

"It's true," Mickey testified.

"The guy who nearly broke my arm to find out where Jackie was is the April Fool Killer?"

"Yes," Mickey said.

"Jesus. I could've been killed."

"You weren't on his list," I said.

"Neither was Jackie," Mickey noted.

"Did you drive out to see Jackie yesterday?" I asked.

"Yeah. In the afternoon."

"Why did you go out there?"

"She owed me some money. She said she could pay it. So I drove out to get it."

"Did you get it?"

"Well, sure."

"Did you drive her out to a vista point?"

"Yeah. She asked me to. She was meeting somebody out there, she said."

"Did she say who?"

"No."

"Now what did she say? Try to remember," I insisted.

"She didn't say who she was meeting."

"Did you see anyone there?"

"There was one car. An old model."

"What kind?"

"I don't know. Foreign, I think."

"What color?"

"It was dirty. I didn't notice. Except for one thing. It had California plates. But don't ask. I didn't get the license."

"Did you see anyone in it?"

"No."

"She must have said something about this meeting."

"Yeah. She said she was going to get enough money from this
guy to quit the business."

"A customer?"

"Maybe."

I looked at Mickey. "There's a book full of suspects."

"She said this guy was gonna pay through the nose for fuckin'
her."

"Was she angry?"

"Sort of. And pleased. Then she gave me a letter to Express
Mail. She had the envelope ready and everything."

"Did you do it?"

"Sure. She gave me the money for it."

"Where was it going?"

"To a box in San Francisco."

"A name?"

"A Mr. G. Vincent."

"Her father," I said to Mickey. "He would have received it by
now."

"If you believe the ads for the post office."

"Do you remember the box number?"

"No way."

"What about the receipt?" Mickey asked.

"I threw it away. It wasn't anything to me."

"What did she say about this letter?"

"She said this guy was gonna shit a brick when he found out."

"Which guy?"

"The guy she was meeting, I guess. I thought that was who she
meant. But you know, I'm not sure."

"And that's it?"

"She said it would explain things."

"What things?" I asked.

"I don't know. That's all she said."

"And you just left her off there?" I asked.

"Sure. That's what she wanted. She said she'd get a ride back with this guy she was meeting. I didn't know she was gonna end up dead, for Christ's sake."

"She didn't seem scared or worried?" Mickey asked.

"No. Not at all. I think her line of work toughened her up when it came to men."

"I bet," Mickey said.

Joe Coglin came over. More than ten minutes had passed. He wanted to get back to work. No problem. We had all we were going to get.

"Thanks, Sherry," I said.

"I can't believe it about Jackie. She seemed so sure this was going to be the end of it.'"

"She was right," I said.

"I guess so," Sherry said as she turned to go back on stage.

We waved good-bye to Joe.

I called Johnny D. and alerted him to the fact that Gutman had a San Francisco P.O. Box under the name of G. Vincent. I knew the cops wouldn't have any trouble getting the number. They might even get lucky and pick him up collecting his mail. But somehow I doubted it. I added, "You can tell your Reno friends that a showgirl named Sherry Wine at the Silver Bar Casino drove Jackie out to the point yesterday."

"Would you spell that Wine as in a bottle of wine?"

"You win the spelling bee."

"Thanks, Jeremiah," he said.

"Are we ready to fly back?" Mickey asked when I got off the phone.

"Sure. My guess is that Gutman is now in the Bay Area."

The plane was practically empty. A good place to talk over the case.

"Who do you thing she was meeting?" Mickey asked. "If it wasn't her father."

"She could have been blackmailing any one of the men on that list of clients."

"That's a long list.

"We get to subtract the dead ones."

"Cute."

"One obvious matter," I said. "What was in that letter to Gutman?"

"It must have been something she wanted him to know about the guy she was meeting. So she couldn't have been meeting Gutman."

"Sounds like that to me. Unless she wasn't expecting Gutman and he showed up. That seems to be the way he works."

"Damn. What do we have?" she asked.

"A long list of names.

16

We got back late Saturday afternoon. I was surprised to find the Chief at work so close to the dating hour.

"No luck with the camcorder," Chief Moses said as he looked up from a thick file he was leafing through. It wasn't anything I recognized but I didn't ask. The Chief has been known to help out his Indian friends who cannot afford our fees at a discount—free. "And one more thing. Cook was released from jail."

"On bail?" I asked.

"Charges were dropped."

"At least the Yellow Suns can continue the interrogation they began."

"Our MIA has disappeared."

"No trail for the Great Tracker to follow?"

"Not yet."

"We've got some other things to discuss," Mickey said.

The three of us settled into my office while we went over our latest trip to Tahoe for the Chief.

"It could have been that Gutman was no longer able to take the shame," he said.

"Nancy Gutman doesn't believe it," I said.

"Ted Bundy's mother thought he was a swell kid, too," Mickey noted. Then she added, "You realize we haven't met your client face-to-face yet."

"True," I said.

"What are you hiding?" Mickey asked.

"Nothing," I said.

"Then we should meet the lady," Mickey concluded.

"You're right. It would be a good idea if we all sat down together."

"We might pick up on some things you may have missed, Jeremiah," the Chief said.

"Hey, anything's possible."

"But this is likely," Mickey tossed in.

I called Nancy and asked her to come over for a home-cooked dinner with my partners. After she accepted my invitation, I sent out for Chinese. We got some beer and wine out of the small downstairs refrigerator.

It took her less than fifteen minutes to come over.

She looked very sexy in a tight cotton sweater, hip-hugging black slacks, and sling-back heels.

I introduced everyone and I repeated for Nancy's sake what we had learned up in Tahoe. "It's not much," I admitted.

"Not if you're trying to prove Vincent didn't do it," she said.

"How can you be so sure he didn't," Mickey asked.

Nancy hesitated. "Because he called me. He was practically incoherent. Just kept asking, why would I kill my own daughter? He didn't talk about the other killings."

"Is that the first time you heard from him?" Chief Moses asked.

"Yes. I swear it."

"Where was he?" I asked.

"He said that he was in the city. But that's all."

The delivery boy arrived with our meals. I paid him and carried the food into my office.

"This is home cooking?" Nancy asked.

"For Jeremiah, it is," the Chief explained.

"I was busy," I apologized. I spread everything out on my desk and we went at it—except for Mickey. While we ate, Nancy kept insisting that her son would not have lied to her about Jackie. No matter what else he did.

The Chief and Mickey looked skeptical. Which I could understand considering Gutman's record so far. But I tended to believe her. There were too many holes in the evidence.

"When Nancy went to use the bathroom, Mickey said to me, "She's very attractive."

"For someone her age," I noted.

"For a squaw," Chief Moses said, "of any age."

"Aerobics does it for her."

"That and a carrot a day diet," Mickey noted. This from a woman who didn't eat a thing tonight.

"Not from the way she ate the Kung Pao chicken and the Moo Shu beef," Chief Moses noted.

"Do you think Gutman killed his daughter?" the Chief asked me.

"No."

"How do we prove it?" Chief Moses asked.

"I don't know. But we can start by trying to find him."

"Good luck," Mickey said.

Nancy came back and sat on the couch with Mickey. The Chief and I were sitting on reasonably comfortable client chairs. The trash can was full of white cartons. It was growing dark outside but we hadn't switched on the inside lights yet and the room was full of soft gray shadow.

"This seems like the right time of day for a little reflection," I said.

"Reflect," the Chief said as he stretched out his legs.

"I'll try. Some of this may fit in directly with Nancy's case and some may not. But I'm getting to believe it's all tied together somehow. We have two threads here. There's the General Bloodhart protection and extortion racket, which is using former MIA's to terrorize Vietnamese businessmen. On the other hand, we have Vincent Gutman, another returned MIA, running around with his own motives. Maybe he was supposed to be part of the same Bloodhart operation, but he turned into a loose cannon on the deck."

"What does that mean for him?" Nancy asked.

"It may mean he's making Bloodhart very unhappy."

"Which could be very harmful to his health," Chief Moses said.

"What do we do?" Nancy asked.

"I have to give Curtis a call," I said. I explained about Curtis and the Dragon Seeds to Nancy, then got Curtis on the line and told him that I wanted him putting out the word on the street that he had a vet looking to get into the Bloodhart organization. "If we couldn't get to Bloodhart, maybe he could come to us," I told him.

"Ain't gonna tempt my guys with that," Curtis protested.

"Just put out the word. I'll supply the manpower." I hung up and looked at the Chief.

"So you want to cast me as a Vietnam vet."

"You'd be perfect. Love to see you dressed in jungle fatigues and army boots."

"I do not like it."

This looks like the only way. We get you to be part of his extortion gang."

"Do I get to wrestle Agent Orange?"

"You get to wrestle Rambo," Mickey said.

We all laughed, except for Nancy. Her family's tragedy had to be weighing on her. She got up and said, "I appreciate this chance to meet with all of you, but I really have to leave."

I walked her to the front door. She embraced me and I hugged her back. She put her head on my shoulder and sobbed quietly. I didn't say anything. I just let her cry it all out. Things didn't look good for her son. And I knew they were only going to get worse.

"Nice lady," Mickey said.

"Yeah. How come you didn't eat?" I asked.

"I have a late dinner date with Glenn," she explained.

"And I have a date to see a John Wayne Western," Chief Moses announced.

"What about the camcorder?" I asked.

"I will check it in the morning," he promised.

"Especially make sure it's still there."

Mickey and the Chief left. Alone again. I decided to wander down to Japantown, which was only four blocks away from the office. I went into the Japantown Bowl and watched the Brunswick automatic scoring machines at work. One less human chore; one less chance to cheat your way to a 200 game. I walked back along Post Street with its two radically different sides: things "wabi," the old, on one side; things "sabi," the new, on the other. I went "sabi" and found a video store. I rented *Rambo*, hoping that Stallone would give me some ideas about how to deal with General Bloodhart.

It turned out that I got a copy that was dubbed in Japanese. What a way to spend a Saturday night.

Sunday had to be better. That's what I thought, at least.

It got off to a good enough start. I beat my San Francisco State competition on the courts and had a good workout in my gym. In the middle of my shower, the Chief came barging in yelling, "Good news! I have our Condom Vandal in action. The vending machine was demolished on camera last night."

"Let's hope someone recognizes the guy," I said as I toweled dry quickly and pulled on a pair of pants.

Half-dressed, I went downstairs with the impatient Chief to watch the tape. He fast-forwarded it until we got the action we wanted. We stared at the Condom Vandal in freeze-frame. Then we ran that section in slow motion.

"Do you see it?" Chief Moses the eagle-eyed one asked.

"I see some average-looking guy of about forty with a crewcut and wearing a black coat working on a vending machine with a crowbar. Now we've got to identify him."

"Look at his neck, Jeremiah."

I saw it. A white collar was just barely visible. A Roman collar. "He's a priest!"

The Chief was ready to leave with the tape for the Archdiocese Chancery Office, appropriately located on Church Street, which he assumed would be open on Sunday.

"It is their one business day in the week," he declared.

"Maybe," I said. I also didn't doubt that he would try to find the Archbishop no matter what. "But I'm glad you wrapped it up. We've got to concentrate on getting you into the Bloodhart operation."

To set that up I needed some help from Dr. Elgin Koyota. After Chief Moses left, I called Koyota, but he wasn't at the lab. I tried Curtis but no one at Dragon Seeds knew where he was. I switched on the TV, hoping there would be some tennis matches on the Cable Sports Network I subscribe to. Instead of live tennis, they were showing reruns of the 1984 Summer Olympics in L.A. I was about to turn it off when there was a cut to a local news bulletin. A maid going in to clean up a motel room had discovered a body that police tentatively identified as suspected April Fool Killer Vincent Gutman.

"Now back to the games," the talking head said.

I switched to our local channels, looking for more information. I got it from a pretty black-haired Oriental woman on channel five.

Reporters were swarming around outside of a downtown motel. They were trying to get somebody to say something. I saw Chang pass by with a "No comment." Johnny D. brushed aside a microphone that had been rudely shoved into his face. The reporters finally got a fish to bite when they went after Dr. Koyota. I remembered what the WAC had said about his loving publicity. He lived up to her billing. The doctor, dressed in a three-piece suit, kept trying to get his left profile on camera. I had to admit it was his better side.

"The preliminary identification is that the dead man is one Vincent Gutman, until recently believed to be an MIA of the Vietnam War," he said on camera.

The questions flew at him about the April Fool Killer.

"The dead man apparently committed suicide."

They tried to get more out of him but someone from the D.A.'s Office hauled him away before he could give any of his theories on the case and compromise the investigation. With no one else willing to talk, the station cut from the woman reporter and returned to its regularly scheduled programming.

I went outside and stood on the porch. I didn't want to call Nancy again with more bad news. I heard the phone ring inside the office. I left it to the answering machine and started up the hill to the park. I stopped at Sacramento Street and walked over to the house that Arthur Conan Doyle once lived in. The building was made of white stone. It was two stories high with a second-story balcony overlooking the street. The narrow building was decorated with elaborate stone carvings in relief above and around the front windows. But it was the shining gold plaque that attracted me. It hung above a potted bush and read, "This house, built in 1881, was once occupied by Sir Arthur Conan Doyle." It didn't say for how long and it didn't say what, if anything, he wrote while here. But that didn't seem important. I studied the plaque and wished for inspiration. I crossed the street and sat in the park on a wooden bench, I'd have to call Nancy Gutman. Maybe she had heard already and I wouldn't be breaking the news. Or maybe she hadn't and I would be breaking her heart.

I didn't have to call her. She was sitting in her Mercedes smoking, parked across the street from the office.

I came up to the car and she lowered the electric window the rest of the way down.

"You heard?" I asked. From the shattered look on her face, I knew she had. Her eyes were red but tearless. At least for now.

"It's over," she said as she took a deep drag.

"Yes."

"But that doesn't mean you're done." She put out the cigarette in the car ashtray. There was hardly room for another butt.

"Why not?"

"I don't believe he killed his daughter and I don't believe he committed suicide."

"It would follow," I said.

"No. Find the truth." She started her car.

"This is costing you a lot of money."

"I don't give a damn. I can afford it. Find out what the hell really happened."

"It may be just what the police say."

"Or maybe not."

I relented. "I'll stay on it," I said. "But I can't promise anything."

"Who can?" she asked as she pulled away from the curb. No tears. Just a woman in pain.

Johnny D. was at the precinct house when I called and I invited myself over to see him. I found him drinking a cup of coffee at his desk. As I came up he put the cup down and said, "This would work better in my car than in my gut. Want some?"

"No, thanks. I only use synthetic motor oil."

"You want something?"

"Chang here?"

"He knew you were comin' and decided to split."

"Smart man," I said and sat down.

"Hey, the man doesn't wanna see or hear or smell any evil."

"Close enough. What have you got on Gutman?"

He went over some of the same stuff I picked up from Koyota on the news. But he added, "Stein identified Gutman as the killer."

"No surprise," I said.

"But that suicide stuff was bullshit."

"Don't tell me, Gutman was holding the gun in his right hand and he was a lefty."

"That's only on 'Perry Mason.' The gun was in the proper hand but the fingers were loose. You can't put a gun into a dead man's hand and get the fingers to grip tight. And the preliminary paraffin test shows that Gutman didn't fire a gun."

"What about tracing the weapon?"

"Looks impossible. One of those with the serial number burned off with acid. We can't bring it back up."

"Could it have been Gutman's?"

"I doubt it. When he tried to kill that lawyer and was getting his ass kicked, he didn't go for a gun."

"Yeah." That wasn't conclusive but it was probable. I could tell Nancy the good news. She was right. Vincent had most likely been murdered. If that could pass for good news. "Did the Crime Scene Unit come up with something simple like an Express Mail envelope mailed to a Mr. G. Vincent?"

"We got that from the wastebasket. It was empty. We're checking it for prints."

"The killer took the contents," I said.

"Maybe, but why toss the envelope where it can be found?"

"There is that. I've got another idea; Gutman was a loose cannon." I told Johnny D. everything I knew about General Bloodhart and the MIA's—which wasn't much. "Gutman was drawing attention to whatever was going on. They couldn't control him, so they eliminated him."

"You got any evidence?"

"Not yet."

Johnny sighed and made a notation on a pad. "I'll run a check on this Bloodhart guy. It makes some sense."

"Thanks, Johnny." I started to get up.

"We're gonna go with the apparent suicide story for a while to lull our killer into security."

"I'll explain the situation to the mother. She won't give you a problem."

"She better not. I know who to blame."

I left the precinct house. On the walk back, I thought about the letter Jackie had sent him and what might have been in it. It seemed to me it was the key to a lot of things.

I called Nancy from my flat. "You were right. Vincent was murdered."

There was a long silence.

"Can I come over?"

"Yes," I said.

"Have you eaten?" she asked.

"No."

"I'll stop for some pizza."

"Okay."

In less than an hour she appeared with a large sausage and green pepper pizza, which we took upstairs to eat in the kitchen. I got out a Henry's for me and red wine for her. I went over the police story she would hear.

"So you have to play along," I said.

"Of course." she refilled her wine glass.

I went over my discussion with Johnny D. "What could Jackie have sent him?" I asked.

"I don't know." She put down the one piece she was eating.

I put the rest of the pizza in the refrigerator and sat next to her on the couch in my living room. I started back on the case when she said, "Make love to me."

She put her arms around my neck and kissed me hard on the lips. I felt her breasts pressing me. I wrapped my arms around her.

She pulled her face back and said, "This is a new era. And I'm uncomfortable as hell with it." She paused. "You're not a bisexual, are you?"

"No."

"You want to hear about me?" she asked.

"Sure." The conversation was cooling things down. Which was fine with me.

"I had a monogamous relationship with my husband until his death; I have been celibate ever since."

We looked at each other and started to laugh.

"I sound ridiculous," she said.

"You don't want me to make love to you," I said.

There was a long pause. "I want you to hold me. Please."

I held her. For a long time. Finally she said, "Thank you, Jeremiah. I needed that ."

"And that's all you needed."

"No." She paused. "I could use a drink. Plain, please, not Limonaya."

I got her a plain vodka. She drank it right down.

"I'd better be going," she said. She laughed but there were tears suspended in her eyes. She got out the door before I could see them fall.

I went back upstairs, got myself a cold slice of pizza and a Henry's, and tried to get back into my Travis McGee. But I couldn't concentrate. Too many loose ends; too many pieces that didn't fit; too much still to do.

17

I got up early Monday morning, went through my tennis, free weights, and calisthenic ritual, and called Dr. Koyota. He was in.

"You were really impressive on TV yesterday," I said.

"Thank you."

"We need an MIA ID for the Gutman case to give a man a cover."

"Did Mickey see me?"

"Of course. She was very impressed. Will you help us?"

"I will get back to you with an identity you can use."

Flattery and Mickey will get you anything.

It was still very early. I took a cable car downtown. I got off as close as I could to the Tenderloin. I wanted to put some friendly pressure on Curtis.

I had to pound on the door of the Dragon Seeds headquarters to get someone to let me in. There were a few men sleeping on cots in the game room. Curtis was in back, sleeping on a single bed in what looked like a windowless pantry next to the kitchen.

"What is this, man? I'm sleepin'," he complained when I shook him awake.

"You were sleeping. Now you're talking. What do you hear about General Bloodhart?"

"Too early," he tried to turn over on his side.

"The sun's out."

"Shee-it," he said as he rubbed his eyes. "Don't see it back in here."

"What's been happening?"

He sat up in bed. He was wearing olive drab underwear to sleep in. "I put out the word on the street, like you said. We got some nibbles. Seems like this General Bloodhart is usin' troops to extort money from Vietnamese here in California."

"I know that. But we can't get a lead on him."

"There be more to Bloodhart than this racket."

"Like what?" I asked.

"Guys are talkin' 'bout bringin' back MIA's from Nam."

"How?"

"Claim is he gets 'em out by droppin' balloons on the Vietnamese countryside offering rewards for American MIA's."

"And that works?"

"So he claim. But I hear different. Bloodhart's been sendin' troops over there."

"Who are these troops?"

"Hard to say. Some a the MIA's, for sure. Mercenaries. Maybe some psycho vets. Same guys runnin' the racket."

"Who'd you talk to?" I asked.

"Nobody. Know what I mean? Nobody who'll talk to you." He got out of bed and dug out a Camel from his pants pocket and lit up. He coughed. "First cough a the day." He sat on the edge of the bed and smoked.

"Anything else on Bloodhart himself?"

"Who knows? Man served in Vietnam, I hear. Call hisself a general. Jus' like in the South Vietnamese Army. Everybody's a fuckin' general or better."

"But he's been getting out MIA's?"

"I keep sayin' that. You deaf?"

"It's just hard to believe. For one thing, he needs big money for that kind of enterprise. You don't get a private army cheap."

"That's why you need an extortion racket, man." The pantry was full of smoke. Even Curtis began to wave it away. He crushed out the cigarette and swore at it.

"What about the government?" I asked.

"Don't know."

"Let me use your phone." I called Koyota. It was a long shot but I hoped he'd got right on it. He gave me the name, rank, and serial number I needed. The Chief would be transformed into Private First Class Abraham Mosby, listed as missing during the Tet offensive. I thanked Koyota profusely and complimented him on his fast work. We, Mickey and I, are very pleased, I said. He sent his regards to the lady.

I had enough to go on. I gave Curtis what I had from Koyota. I told him exactly what I wanted spread about Chief Moses so it could get to Bloodhart. But I told him to wait until he heard from me.

"No problem," Curtis said as he pulled on a pair of pants.

Yes, there was a problem. But it was mine. I would have to convince the Chief to buy into a plan that no longer just involved local extortion but could also include a privately financed invasion of Vietnam. With Abraham Mosby at the point.

Back at the office, I found Mickey and the Chief waiting for me. They listened while I called Johnny D. and gave him everything I had on Bloodhart from Curtis. Johnny wasn't that impressed but he agreed it was worth pursuing.

"So that is where you have been," Chief Moses said.

"Tell me about your adventures in the chancery," I said.

Before the Chief could say a word, my watch alarm went off, reminding me that I had to move my car for the Monday morning street sweeping.

"That alarm is saving you a lot in towing charges," Mickey said as I rushed to the door. "Credit due to..."

"You," I agreed as I raced out.

When I came back, my partners were sitting on my office couch drinking coffee. I poured myself a cup.

"Back to your chancery adventure," I said.

"I met the Archbishop. A very courteous gentleman. I showed him the videotape and he recognized the Condom Vandal immediately. He said the man was a parish priest who had a history of homophobic behavior. Apparently, this priest believes that AIDS is God's plague sent to rid Earth of the abomination of homosexuality. He sees condoms as a human challenge to the divine plan. He was recently arrested for shoplifting them in a local drugstore.

That was covered up. The Archbishop asked that I not go to the police and he would guarantee that these attacks would stop."

"Did you agree?" Mickey asked.

"That is all my client wanted. Plus money to repair the damaged machines."

"So?"

"So we settled on the amount my client had requested. The Archbishop wrote a check and called the parish where our vandal priest works. He was saying mass. The Archbishop assured me that the priest would be in his office that afternoon and in a psychiatric hospital for treatment that evening. What more could we ask for?"

"Nice work," I said.

"My client thought so. And so did the Archbishop. He asked for my card. He said the archdiocese often has a need for a discreet and reasonable private investigator."

I looked at Mickey. "That would be something different." I said to the Chief, "But right now you don't have a case."

"I would like to take a few days off. Maybe take the houseboat along some inland waterways."

"I have something else in mind for you, Chief," I said.

"Smoke out Bloodhart."

"Right."

The red light on my desk was blinking. I checked the video scanner. Our regular messenger, the young girl with the dark hair and oversized glasses, was at the door.

"Looks like we're back in the juror profile business."

Mickey went to the door and got the packet. We read the cover memo together. This time it was a major civil suit about the transmission of AIDS to a female heterosexual by a male bisexual who apparently knew he had the disease.

"This one is for Mickey."

"Thanks," she said. The consulting firm had a list of questions we were to answer for each prospective juror. I wondered what kind of person the psychologists thought would be inclined to ignore this male's lack of responsibility. I scanned the questions.

"Seems like they're looking for conservative matrons who would see the woman as a whore and gay men who would be inclined to support confidentiality," I said.

"I think it's a lost cause," she said, "no matter who they put up there."

"We get paid whether they win or lose. That's the beauty of it."

"I'd better get right on it." She picked up her camera and note-book and left.

After a few moments of silence, Chief Moses asked, "Did Bloodhart make contact?"

"Not yet."

"So?"

"So I want you to go undercover at the Dragon Seeds to wait for a contact."

"If it does not come?"

"It'll come."

"Why would Bloodhart be interested?"

"Because of your cover."

"Tell me about it."

"You were an MIA for years. Held in a small village in the north. You finally escaped on your own. You came out of there with an intense hatred for the Vietnamese and the desire to go back in there and kick some ass and free the rest of the MIA's."

"Why would he belive this?"

"Because I have an MIA identity for you. Right from Dr. Koyota. You will be Abraham Mosby, missing since the Tet offensive."

Chief Moses walked around the room. He looked out of my win-dow. He shook his head at the dying plants. This was his ritual.

"Curtis will set you up with the cover."

"I do not know."

"Curtis and I will give you everything you need. And he'll give you so much history, you'll think you actually fought and were cap-tured in Vietnam. He'll also explain how you came to escape."

"There must be an easier way to smoke out this Bloodhart."

"If there is, we haven't found it. He's got protection and maybe from some heavy hitters. There is something I have to tell you. I learned from Curtis today that General Bloodhart is looking for some mercenaries to go into Vietnam to pull out MIA's."

"Hell, no. I won't go!" the Chief chanted.

"You won't really have to go there. Not once we get to Bloodhart."

"What is our objective, Jeremiah?"

"Wrap up a case for our client, Nancy Gutman."

"That is not enough."

"Stop what Bloodhart is doing to the Vietnamese in the city. Maybe bring some of his MIA's back to the world. They're still prisoners, it seems to me. Only Bloodhart's the jailer."

I sat quitely while the Chief paced. Finally he nodded. "What do I do?"

"Curtis is waiting for you."

"Can I have today off? You know. To spend the day with my woman before I go off to war."

"What the hell. That'll give me time to get your fake ID documents made up. I'll call Curtis and tell him to expect you tomorrow. He can start putting the word out on you. And one more thing, Chief, you need camouflage gear."

"I will take my woman shopping in the army/navy store."

"Woman have a name?" I asked.

"Not to you."

"Good luck, Chief."

"Final request. When the oil stock hits five, sell." He gave me his broker's number and left for R&R and a new identity.

I called a guy we had an account with who could forge anything and ordered the Chief some fake ID's and dog tags with his MIA name to be sent to the Dragon Seeds. We kept recent photos on file with the man so he could get anything from a driver's license to a passport ready for us in a day. I called Curtis and let him know what to expect. I hoped we had the perfect staked bait to catch a Bloodhart.

Unfortunately, we were not the only ones in the trapping business.

18

By Wednesday, May 11, Mickey had completed a record number of juror profiles and the Chief was undercover at the Dragon Seeds.

I spent some time at the precinct house trying to pick up a lead on either the Jackie Gutman killing or the Vincent Gutman killing. The police were viewing the former as the work of Gutman, the latter as a murder by person or persons unknown. Suicide had been ruled out by the Coroner, so the story was now public information.

I cornered Johnny D. "What about Bloodhart? Any leads?"

"He's got friends in high places. He's pretty much a political untouchable unless we got something solid on him."

"What if Gutman was the loose cannon in his operation?"

"It's not gonna be Bloodhart himself who goes into a motel room and blows Gutman's brains out."

"I know that. But you can't just write Bloodhart off."

"We're not. We're just not gettin' anywhere with him yet."

"What do you mean by that?"

"We can't find the sonofabitch."

"What do you have so far on the Gutman murder?"

Johnny glanced uneasily over at Chang, who was behind the glass wall of his office.

"*Nada*. Nothing. No one saw anybody. Nobody heard anything," Johnny said.

"How about the maid?"

"She's a Flip with no English. We had to get an interpreter. It didn't help. Nobody knows nothin'."

"Any calls from the motel room?"

"This was some sweet place. No phones in the room. No TV. No soap. One towel."

"What about a different angle, Johnny? What if there was a connection that we don't see? What if whoever killed Jackie also killed Gutman?"

"Who?"

"I wish I knew."

"What about a motive?"

"A client she was blackmailing."

"It's possible. But we'd need a tie to Gutman. Somebody hunted him down."

"Which brings us back to General Bloodhart."

"Which keeps us going in a circle. I got a report to finish. I'll let you know if we get anything on Bloodhart. And you do the same."

"Of course." I got up, went down the metal steps, and returned my visitors badge to the desk sergeant.

I walked over to the nearby Burger King and ordered a Whopper, onion rings, and a Diet Coke. While I ate, my mind kept going around in the same circle it had gone around with Johnny.

I spent the afternoon riding from poker parlor to poker parlor, hoping to get at another Bloodhart extortionist. My final stop was the Chew grocery. I came up empty handed.

Back at the office, Mickey, who had been working on the juror profiles, said, "I'm getting sick of work. Let's play mixed doubles tonight."

So that night we played more mixed doubles with Glenn and his ex-wife Gloria. Thanks to her reflexes at the net, she and I won again. Glenn reminded me of the singles match we had next Wednesday night.

"I wouldn't forget that," I said and winked at Mickey. He didn't know the stakes we were playing for. And he didn't know that day happened to be my birthday. Taurus the bull. Taurus the stubborn. Whatever.

As we were walking into the clubhouse he asked me, "Are you going to run the Bay to Breakers this Sunday?" It sounded like a challenge.

"No way." Challenges like that I could ignore.

The ten-kilometer race was an annual San Francisco event. Take a few world-class runners and put them out ahead of approximately 100,000 rowdy joggers and you have the Bay to Breakers. The attraction is that the majority are running in costumes, most as individuals but some as multi-person centipedes. Last year the best individual costume was a man dressed as an ostrich followed by a guy with a baby carriage strapped to his back. In the centipede category a top competitor was the ten-foot condom costume.

"Why not? I am. And how about you, Mickey? Will you run with me?"

She didn't answer.

"Destroys the knees," I said.

"That's a lame excuse."

"Don't get too tired for our match on Wednesday," I said, ignoring his dig. It was easy to do. Besides hurting my knees, running bores me to death.

"Don't worry. Mickey, will you run with me?"

"I don't think so," she said.

"Come on," he insisted.

"I don't know."

"You'll love it. I used to run with Glenn," Gloria interjected. "We once ran as part of a fifty-two person deck of cards."

"No thanks," Mickey concluded.

"I was going to get us into a twelve-pack of beer centipede."

"Especially no thanks."

"But I promised to bring a partner."

"I'll run with you," Gloria said.

Mickey and I exchanged looks.

"Fine," Glenn said.

We sat down at the bar.

On Thursday, the Chief's oil stock hit five and I called his broker and sold. On Thursday we also got two new clients. The Catholic Archbishop and a Fundamentalist preacher.

I explained when the Archbishop called that the Chief was on assignment and not available.

"He seemed a very discreet and reasonable individual."

"We have others," I assured him, lifting a line from our local real estate agents.

"I don't want to discuss this over the phone."

"Our clients never do."

He made an appointment, not for himself, but for one of his assistants who would be coming over in an hour.

Mickey got back from some early morning juror-profile research just in time to be presented as another discreet operator to the young priest who arrived a few minutes after her.

The young man was frail with bluish skin, large dark sunken eyes, deeply hollowed cheekbones, and, in marked contrast, full reddish lips. He looked like a Renaissance painting of a martyred saint. His hands and feet seemed very large for the rest of his rather small body. He wasn't much more than five-six and one hundred twenty pounds. His best feature was a tangle of thick black hair that was so shiny, it looked like a wig, and so high, it added inches to his height.

He introduced himself as Father Peter Francis Morgan, personal secretary to the Archbishop.

We all settled into my office. He accepted the offer of coffee and requested decaffeinated.

"This is a very sensitive subject. There have been rumors of child abuse in a certain elementary parochial school." He stopped, looked around, seemed unable to continue.

"Please don't worry, Father. We'll exercise the utmost discretion," I promised.

"We'd like them investigated." He paused. "You see Mr. St. John, Miss Farabaugh, these are not charges, just rumors. At least at this point. But we must be prudent. There is always the fear of the bad publicity, not to mention lawsuits by the parents."

"Of course."

"Can you do it?" he asked.

"Do you have a suspect?" Mickey asked.

"I wouldn't call him a suspect..."

"The person about whom the rumors are circulating," she said.

"Yes."

"If there is evidence of a crime, the police will have to be notified," I said.

He sank back into the couch. "We understand that."

"Are the children behind the rumors?" I asked.

"No. No child has come forward."

"Where are these rumors starting?" Mickey asked.

"In the faculty. The Archbishop received an anonymous letter from a faculty member. A preliminary investigation conducted by myself suggested that while there was talk about this teacher, there was no evidence that he molested a child. But the Archbishop felt we needed a professional."

"The Archbishop must have felt that you uncovered enough to warrant a full investigation," Mickey said.

"Perhaps." He took a sip of his coffee.

"Is he a priest?" Mickey asked suddenly.

"No. A layman. But with an excellent teaching record in several private schools, I might add."

"Did he change jobs frequently?" I asked.

"Not frequently. But more than usual, I admit. That is a bad sign." Father Peter Francis finished his coffee. "So Mr. St. John, will you take the case?"

I looked at Mickey.

"The juror profiles are nearly done," she said.

"We'll take the case. I'm assigning Mickey to it. She's one of our best."

Father Peter Francis looked relieved. "I feel like I've just been to confession."

He looked like it, too. "You'll have to give us some detailed backgrounds," I said.

"Of course."

Mickey offered him more coffee and he accepted. As he sipped his fresh cup he gave us the name of the teacher, the names of the students about whom the rumors were circulating, and the names of the schools he had worked at previously.

"Now we need an approach," I said.

"Get me some time alone with those kids," Mickey said.

"That can be arranged during recess. When do you want this done?" Father Peter Francis Morgan asked.

"If this is child abuse, yesterday," Mickey said.
"Would you be ready for tomorrow?"
"Fine."
"I'll call the school in the Archbishop's name."
"Good."
"At noon, then?" the priest asked.
"I'll be there. All I need is a small empty classroom."
"Consider it done." Father Peter Francis finished his second cup of coffee and, after we settled on the agency fee, cheerfully left to return to the Chancery and report to his boss.
"Do you know what the hell you're doing?" I asked Mickey.
"I hope so. Now I've got to pick up some supplies."
"What kind of supplies?"
"You'll see. Remember, I'm one of your best," she smiled mischievously, waved, and was gone.
A half hour later, the father called, confirming the arrangements for Mickey.

Mickey had not returned when I was faced with our second religious client of that Thursday. This one, however, was much less ingenuous than the father. This one was pissed off.
He puffed around the office, muttering about thieves, divine retribution, and fire and brimstone, his broad red face getting redder and broader. I resisted the impulse to push him into a chair and ask what in God's name was bothering him. I chose to let him play it out. He would pay for the time so I could be patient.
He had perfect white hair and matching fluffy eyebrows. It looked like the top of his head had been dipped in cotton candy. His cheeks were an apple red, a creation less of emotion than of makeup. He had eyes so blue, they looked like glass. He was over six-three, with what looked like a firm body beneath a white wool suit. I had seen the man once on TV. I was switching channels and got hooked when I saw him curing a man of tennis elbow right there on television for only a thousand dollar contribution to the Church of the Second Coming—Western Rite. Not a bad deal if it got the guy back out on the court. I had to admit that on TV Reverend Kent Starborn, aptly Hollywood named, was an impressive man. And at least he wasn't threatening to die unless he raised ten million dollars for his church.

"What thieves are you talking about?" I asked when my patience ran out.

"I don't appreciate being blackmailed by you and your cohorts," he fumed at me.

"Blackmail? Cohorts?" I laughed. "Sit down, Reverend," I offered. "Care for something for the nerves?"

"I accept no hospitality from a blackmailer."

"Suit yourself. Why do you think I'm blackmailing you?"

"Come now. I am not a fool."

"I don't know what you're talking about."

"Don't play games with Kent Starborn. I'll pay for the videotapes. But you'll live to regret what you did to that poor woman."

"Look. Start from the beginning. Or get out of here."

"I was contacted by men who claim they have a compromising videotape of my wife. They are willing to sell me the master and all copies of the tape for $25,000."

"What's this got to do with me?"

He glared at me. "They insisted that I use you to deliver the money and make the trade."

"And that makes me a blackmailer?"

"Yes."

I raised my voice. "That's idiotic. If I was involved, you wouldn't know my name."

"Possibly. Possibly not."

"Think about it, Reverend. Would I expose myself like this?"

He sat down. "I don't know what to think. My wife . . ."

"Did your wife admit to this . . . indiscretion?"

"She confessed it and I forgave her."

"Big of you."

He leaned forward, his eyes pinning mine. "I am a man of the cloth."

"And of TV evangelism."

"What do you mean?"

"I mean you want to protect yourself and your church."

"Not me. Her. It won't hurt me or my church."

"It wouldn't exactly help. These days TV preachers are right down there in the public's confidence with lawyers, child molesters, and mass murderers. You guys don't need another sex scandal. Even if it's your wife instead of you. Anything like this cuts contributions. You know it and I know it."

"I don't much care for you, St. John."

"And I wouldn't go to your church on a bet."

"So we understand each other. Will you make the trade?" He was subdued.

"I'll do it. Frankly, I'm more than a little curious about why I was named." I told him my hourly fee.

"Agreed."

"What do they want me to do?"

"They are going to call tonight to give me further instructions. And one other thing. This must be strictly confidential."

"Of course. That's how I always work."

He left me with a retainer but without shaking hands. Who the hell could these blackmailers be? I didn't have much time to think about it. Mickey showed up with a bag full of puppets and other supplies.

"What is this?"

"I'm going to put on a puppet show for each child allegedly involved, to demonstrate child abuse."

"And that's going to nail this guy?"

"Maybe. Now watch. And she played out an example with hand puppets in a wooden box of a stage complete with a curtain. "So, Jeremiah, what do you think?"

"You're explicit enough. If a boy or girl's been molested, you have a good chance they'd have a strong reaction."

"That's what I want."

"I'm impressed. Where'd you get this routine?"

"I used to do this for elementary school kids when I was a cop."

"Why didn't you ever tell me?"

"How many little kids have we had for clients before?"

"We're not working for the little kids," I said.

"Oh, yes I am," she said.

There was no answer to that.

I told her about our new client and his problems. She reminded me that there was a piece on him in a recent issue of a magazine we subscribed to. I dug it out. Reverend Kent Starborn was a radical right-wing preacher who wanted to keep America for Americans. He wanted the army at the borders, Latin Americans deported, Marielitos returned to Cuba, and Asians sent home. Now I understood the name of his church. The Church of the Second Coming—Western Rite. The Lord Jesus was coming for us in the West (White) and not for anyone Eastern (Yellow) or Southern (Brown and Black.) Where did the man put New York or San Francisco in his theology? I hoped this guy had a tape of his wife with a Mexican and an Asian. Serve him right.

"This is some man of God," I said.

"These days guys like him are the rule, not the exception," she responded.

19

The next day was Friday, the thirteenth day of the month. A disc jockey on the radio was broadcasting from a bed which he swore he would not get out of until the day was over. A tempting idea when my morning started with a call from Starborn. He had been contacted last night, as promised. The exchange was scheduled for Monday morning. We would have to wait until Sunday for the site. He hung up just as the Chief arrived, contrary to all instructions, dressed in a Seminole jersey, camouflage pants, and jungle boots.

"Did anyone follow you here?" I asked. "I don't want you to blow your cover."

He gave me a look so scornful it made my scalp tingle. I changed the subject. "Well? How's it going?" I asked.

"It is like living in a smokehouse. I am turning into smoked meat." He sniffed at his arms.

"Other than that problem?"

"I have been thoroughly indoctrinated by Curtis. I even believe I spent six years imprisoned by villagers in Vietnam."

"What about the general?" I asked.

"I have been contacted. The message was to meet a man at a Tenderloin bar. I did. He asked all the questions Curtis prepared me for. From your description, I would say it was the man captured at Chew's grocery."

"Richard Martini. What happens next?" I asked.

"I am supposed to wait."

"They must be checking your identity."

After a workout upstairs and a shower, the Chief reappeared in full camouflage fatigues. I told him I had sold his stocks as he instructed.

"They reached five."

"They went higher today," he said.

"Life is a gamble."

"Thank you, Mr. Dong." The Chief went to wait for General Bloodhart. After he left, I realized I had forgotten to tell him about Mickey's chancery case. Even stranger, Chief Moses had neglected to ask after her. He was feeling the pressure, no matter how much he tried to hide it.

I packed up the juror profiles and called for a messenger. The same young woman with her uniform and oversized glasses arrived by bike.

I called Johnny D. to tell him Bloodhart had made contact with the Chief.

I put what we had on General Bloodhart and his operation in a file. It wasn't much. Time to check him out at the library. It was fifteen blocks south down Van Ness Avenue to the Main City Library in the Civic Center. Unfortunately, the Civic Center was not on a cable car route and the parking would be horrendous at this time of day. I could take a bus but I decided to walk.

It took me about a half hour to reach the library, an imposing building wedged in between the State Building and the Federal Building on McCallister Street across from City Hall.

The computerized data retrieval system was a timesaving marvel. I did a search of references to Bloodhart and got a printout that led me to the few specific issues of newspapers and magazines with information on him. I tracked them down, Xeroxed the articles, and sat down to sift through the pieces.

Despite all the rumors of military adventures in Vietnam, most of the stories concentrated on his program of dropping balloons on the countryside. I did find out that he held the rank of colonel during the Vietnam War, that he had been wounded in action, briefly held captive by the Viet Cong, and that he was one of the bitterest opponents of our military pullout. I couldn't tell exactly where he stood with our current government but he came off sounding like something of a hero who might be involved in covert anticommunist actions. Apparently, he had been promoted to general shortly before he retired from the military. There were some stories of mercenary adventures in Africa which the general denied. There was no mention of a family. He also didn't like being photographed.

When I got back later that afternoon, Mickey was sitting in my office on the couch with her head down. She looked pale and ill.

"How'd it go?"

"They had six children for me. I put on a puppet show for each of them. I could tell it upset some of them. They were getting it. But no one said a thing. I told them if they wanted to talk to me, I would stay in the room."

"What happened?"

"One of the little girls came back and gave me a handprinted note that said, 'Mr. Blummer did just what you showed on that doll to me.'"

"Christ!"

She raised her head and our eyes met. "I asked her some questions and she gave me some of the details. It was sickening. I went to the principal, who immediately suspended Blummer."

"Want a shot of vodka?"

"I do. But a walk in the park would be better."

"Want me to come along?"

"No. I don't think so. Nothing personal."

"I understand."

She went out, leaving me alone with the Bloodhart papers. I went through them again until the Archbishop himself called to express his thanks.

"He'll have to be turned over to the police," I said.

There was a long pause. "Of course," the prelate said.

Mickey returned at four. She went back to work on the computer. That usually made her feel better. I left her alone. She needed to work this out by herself.

Mickey left at five, turning down my offer of dinner.

She said, "I'd be lousy company. I keep thinking about that little girl."

I set all of the security systems in place and went to dinner at my old favorite, Monday's.

When I got back, the marvelous security system, the wonder of the new age of electronics, had been breached. Or so I thought. Someone had broken in and tossed my office files. For a break-in, it was a pretty neat job. Some files were scattered around on the floor but they remained intact. But on my desk lay the empty Bloodhart file. Someone wanted to make it very clear that they were looking for the general's material. I got the message with no problem.

Most incriminating were the notes connecting him to the extortion of money from Vietnamese business operations. Bloodhart must have gotten my name when Hank Chew said it in front of our MIA before he made his escape. The general and I were getting acquainted and I didn't much care for his methods.

Nothing else but the filing cabinets had been broken into. The security system was actually intact. It had not been breached, just circumvented.

I got a flashlight, went into my tangled backyard, and found the marks of a ladder on the dry ground under one of my unbarred second-story windows. There had been a ladder leaning against the empty house next door all day and I had seen a painter around. Now it was gone. I didn't imagine the painter would be back, either. It looked like bars were in order for the second story as well.

"What a day. A perfect Friday the Thirteenth," I shouted to the neighborhood, which responded with its usual indifference.

First thing Saturday, I checked on Mickey. The news of the break-in got her mind off the little girl, at least temporarily.

I called Curtis and got to talk to the Chief, who was still waiting impatiently. I got his litany of complaints about the accommodations at the Dragon Seeds headquarters. I gave him the news about the break-in.

"Anything on my cover in that Bloodhart file?"

"No."

"Are you sure? No mention of Abraham Mosby?"

"Nothing. Hang tough. An old Indian saying," I said.

"Kiss off. Contemporary American saying."

I hung up and called Johnny D. at home. After I exchanged pleasantries with his charming Mexican wife, whose English really was improving, she called her husband to the phone.

"Anything shaking on Bloodhart?" I asked.

"I'll tell you exactly what happened. We were tapping all our sources to find him. Chang got to his contact in the CIA who promised to call him back. Next thing we know, we get a call from the Commissioner."

"So?"

"I told you Bloodhart's got clout."

"What does it translate into?"

"We were told to lay off the general. Drop the whole thing. Seems it's a matter of national security."

"Bullshit."

"Maybe. But the Commissioner got his call direct from Washington. Bloodhart's operation has some powerful supporters. We can't touch him."

"Something stinks as bad as a dead whale on a beach."

"I know. Chang knows. But what could we do?"

"What the hell. Good try, Johnny." I hung up and thought about what a P.I., unhampered by restraints, could do. I spent some of the afternoon drawing a chart that connected the various segments of the case. I had a lot of the pieces. But to what? This wasn't an ordinary puzzle that would come together as a picture. This was more like working with Rubic's Cube.

At that point, I couldn't come up with a single new idea. So I worked out in the gym upstairs and went to the courts to practice my serve. It was only four days to my match with Glenn. Besides, I thought it would help clear my head.

When it didn't, I came back and put the game of the week on TV. I fell asleep in the seventh inning. If it's not the A's or the Giants playing, I can't get too excited.

I was awakened by Mickey, the afternoon newspaper in hand.

"Did you see this?"

I turned off the TV and looked at the article she was pointing at. It was a story on Clinton Blummer, a parochial school teacher who was found hanging in his apartment. The police suspected either suicide or a rare sexual deviation that involved a noose and masturbation. There was no mention of the suspension for child molesting or any police investigation.

She looked around the office. "Now about that break-in. All that was missing was the Bloodhart file?"

"That's it."

"It had to be a warning. We need bars on the second floor."

"Obviously."

I gave her a glass of wine and offered to drive her home. She accepted gratefully.

"I've got some more news." I told her about Bloodhart and Johnny D.

"Does this mean we lay off him?" she asked.

"Just because the CIA wants us to. No way."

"Are you sure it's the CIA?"

"It's everybody's best guess."

"How about that ride home?" she asked.

"Wednesday is the tennis match," I said when we were in the car.

"I know." She gave me a hint of a smile.

"I hope the Bay to Breakers wears him out."

"How do you know I'm rooting for you?"

"Because I'm cuter."

"That's not an objective opinion."

"Because I haven't been married four times. That's an objective fact."

In spite of myself, I watched the Bay to Breakers on Sunday. Some of the costumes almost made it worth it. I was impressed by a hot race between a guy dressed as the Eiffel Tower and a guy dressed as the Transamerica Building. I was rooting for the local landmark when the cameras cut to a guy running as a waiter, complete with a tray of drinks. The waiters I've known should move so fast.

Then incredibly, considering the hordes of runners, I thought I spotted Glenn and Gloria in a twelve-pack of Bud centipede.

I switched channels and caught a few minutes of Starborn making his plea for God and money for his church up in Mendocino County.

Between the race and the Reverend, my breakfast started doing flips in my gut. Time to visit Dragon Seeds headquarters. I took the usual two cable cars downtown and walked over to the Tenderloin. Everyone was awake. Curtis told me that Chief Moses had left yesterday with a thin bearded man in fatigues. Our extortionist Martini, I assumed.

"Where'd they go?"

"Talk to Agent Orange." He gestured toward the kitchen.

Yesterday. I didn't like this. He had made no attempt to contact me. No message on the answering machine. It was possible that he had no access to a phone. The break-in at the office couldn't have compromised the Chief. There was nothing in the Bloodhart file about his going undercover. I had to assume things were going as planned. But that didn't mean I didn't want to know more.

The huge man was in the kitchen eating pancakes. He offered me some and I took him up on it. They turned out to be good.

I told him so.

"From scratch," he said.

"Who did the Chief go off with?" I asked.

"The guy from the grocery store," he said.

"Did you hear them say anything?"

"That Abraham Mosby had checked out."

"Anything else?"

"They were goin' to the jungle," he said as he took a big mouthful of syrup-drenched pancakes.

"There are a lot of jungles," I said as I pushed away my empty plate.

He shrugged. "Want some more pancakes?"

"No. Just an answer."

"Up north." He lowered his head to his plate and started into a second stack of pancakes.

"Could you be a little more specific?"

He cut himself a triangle out of the stack. He held it up on his fork and looked at it. The piece was dripping with syrup and butter. "Mendocino County. That's all I heard."

"Thanks," I said and left.

Mendocino County was rough country. The border was a hundred miles north of the Golden Gate Bridge, straight up the 101 corridor. Across it you entered a war zone that was part of the area known as the "Emerald Triangle," where much of the state's commercial pot was grown. It was where "guerrilla growers" set up their farms in remote areas on public lands and protected them with explosives, bear traps, deadfalls, snares, fishhooks strung at eye level across trails, shotguns, and even attack dogs. It was where the state CAMP program—an acronym for the Campaign Against Marijuana Planting—unleashed helicopters with paramilitary crews to search and destroy the pot fields. It was where the growers were expert not only at protecting their farms on the ground but also at camouflaging them to keep them invisible from the air. It was the closest thing we had to the Vietnam War in California.

It was also a favorite home base for a variety of religions that liked to stay out of the spotlight of San Francisco scrutiny. From Christian monks in monasteries to Buddhists living in their own City of Light complete with the largest temple in North America. Mendocino County was also the home of the Church of the Second Coming—Western Rite.

Suddenly I remembered the pack of matches from a bar in Mendocino County that our grocery store extortionist had used to light his cigarette. Two things at least had clicked together.

I checked the answering machine. Reverend Starborn had called. I dialed the 800 number he gave me and a church secretary transferred my call to him.

"I have further instructions, St. John," he said.

"Do you have the money?"

"Yes." He gave me the details of the switch. It was to take place tomorrow morning at Golden Gate Park. Originally a desert of sand dunes, the park's thousand-plus acres now contained ball fields, bridal paths, and vast expanses of lawn. At night it was an excellent place to commit murder or rape or just dump off a body. But we were meeting in daylight. It sounded routine. But I've been mistaken about things like that before.

"Where in the park?"

"They're going to call tomorrow morning."

"I'll need to take along a camcorder to play the tapes," I said.

"I don't want you looking at my wife's shame, sir."

"I won't be looking at her shame. I'll be checking out the tapes. So bring me a picture of your wife along with the money so I can make sure she's on this tape and they're not selling you some X-rated video starring Candy Barr mooning Miami."

"I don't like it."

"You don't have to like it. Just understand it. It's part of my job to make sure you get what you pay for."

"I told you my wife confessed that she did it."

"That doesn't mean they wouldn't try to screw you twice. They have their eyes fixed on that TV show of yours that pulls in all the money from your flock of believers."

"All right. I'll bring everything over early tomorrow morning."

"Good. By the way. I caught some of your program today."

"Changing your ways?"

"Possibly. I didn't realize it came from Mendocino County. That article on you didn't mention that."

"They were following my Southern California tour."

"Oh."

"Many followers in the south. But Mendocino was the site of my first church."

"Lots of interesting folks up there."

"Some."

"There's a certain general I've been trying to locate."

"Have you tried the Presidio?"

"Thanks for the tip."

20

Reverend Starborn arrived at my office early Monday morning carefully made up, wearing his white wool suit, and trailing a cloud of sweet musky cologne. We skipped the preliminaries.

He had a briefcase he claimed was full of the payoff money. He also had a picture of his wife. Although she was modestly dressed in a high-neck blouse and knee-length A-line skirt, I didn't have any trouble imagining what she would look like naked. Kent Starborn had himself a very beautiful wife.

"I'll recognize her," I said.

"I'm sure you will. She's a very memorable woman."

"I can see that."

"I got their last call this morning. The meeting is to take place at nine-thirty by the Dutch Windmill in Golden Gate Park."

"Right off the Great Pacific Highway. A pretty open area," I noted.

"That's what they said."

I took the briefcase, an old heavy leather piece, and opened the twin locks. It was full of packs of banded bills. I started to count the money.

"It's all there, St. John. Exactly $25,000 dollars."

"I can't take your word for it. It's my ass on the line out there if it's short." I counted it carefully. It was all there.

"Satisfied?"

"Don't take it personally. These guys are going to check it just like I did. They'll count it down to the last hundred."

He started for the door.

"No so fast. Reverend."

"What is it? I want to get back to my wife. She is very upset about all this."

"I don't blame her. But I expect the rest of my fee now."

He counted the amount out in cash, which I appreciated.

"If I ever learn you were part of their blackmail scheme..." he threatened as he turned to exit.

"We went over that. You know better, Reverend."

"Just get the tapes."

When he left, carrying away most of his cloud of sweet cologne, I opened all the windows to try to get rid of the rest.

Mickey arrived a few minutes later. She sniffed the air and asked, "Fly in a couple of pros you met at the Seven Veils Ranch for morning aerobic exercises, Jeremiah?"

"Pretty close. Reverend Starborn fighting the odor of his mortality. Along with the cologne he delivered the cash."

"I'd rather smell that."

"The odor of money."

"When do you make the payoff?" she asked.

I checked my watch. "In an hour and a half at the Dutch Windmill."

Mickey sat down on the couch.

"Let's have some coffee," I said. "I want to go over what we have on Bloodhart so far."

"Fine. If you make the coffee."

"Deal."

I joined her on the couch with our mugs.

"The Chief's gone. Maybe on his way to Vietnam, but I doubt it. More likely he's somewhere in the mountains of Mendocino County. Then there's Starborn with his church in Mendocino. The America-First attitudes, the hatred of immigrants, the right-wing positions, the fervent anticommunism tie them together like Siamese twins."

"They'd love that analogy," Mickey said.

"I hope I get to use it someday."

"Do you think Starborn coming to you was just a coincidence?"

"No. I don't." I looked at my watch. "I've got a job to do."

"It's still early," Mickey said.

"I'm going to get some breakfast."

She got up. "All right. Then let's go. We've got a job to do."

"I can handle this alone."

"You always need backup in this kind of situation," she said, the former cop talking.

"This should be a simple transaction. The money for the tapes."

"In blackmail nothing is simple. You should know that."

I looked at her. "You sold me."

"And you'll throw in breakfast?"

"At Burger King."

She groaned.

"One of the ninety restaurants in our square mile. Take it or leave it."

She took it.

First I stopped at a Union 76 station for gas. When I tried to pay, I couldn't find my credit card.

"Looking for something?" Mickey asked. She was waving the orange and blue card at me. "You gave it to me in Tahoe, remember?"

At Burger King we took our time, even reading the newspaper, while we ate. Clogged with cholesterol, we drove west on Fulton Street across the city to the park. The briefcase and camcorder were in the trunk. I pulled the car into a spot by the seawall across the Great Highway, a hundred yards from the Dutch Windmill. Behind us the Pacific waves were pounding the beach. Salt mist was rising to coat my car. We watched the windmill's arms turn stiffly in the breeze. An image of Don Quixote passed in front of the windshield but I blinked it away. We had about fifteen minutes to go.

"Are we tilting at windmills?" Mickey asked.

So she had conjured up the same image.

"Hope not," I said.

Five minutes later, a black stretch limo with dark smoked windows pulled into the field by the rendezvous spot.

"Let's go," I said.

Mickey checked her latest piece of equipment, a small gun with a lemon-yellow grip that she had ordered from Smith & Wesson. My S&W .38 automatic was in a shoulder holster under my blazer.

I drove slowly across the highway to the park entrance. I stopped about twenty-five yards away from the limo. There were no other cars and nobody else in sight.

We waited, intent on the three side doors of the limo facing us. One of the limo windows glided down and a hand signaled for us to approach.

"Ready?" I asked Mickey.

"I don't like it. The limo doesn't seem right for this kind of deal."

"Maybe the blackmail business is booming these days."

The limo driver impatiently hit his horn.

"Jeremiah, something doesn't feel right."

"What do you suggest?"

"Getting out of here."

"No. Let's get this over with," I said. As it turned out, I should have listened to my partner.

We got out of the T-Bird and I opened the trunk and took out the briefcase and camcorder.

I started to walk across the twenty-five yards of open field to the limo with Mickey behind me. Her gun, although covered by her jacket, was out and ready. In my left hand I had the briefcase and under that arm the camcorder. My right hand was inches away from the gun in my holster. I couldn't wait to find out who these guys were. Business referrals like this I didn't need.

We were about ten yards from the limo when things began to happen at fast-forward speed. The window of the rear door on our side of the limo came down. Just at the moment the alarm that Mickey had set on my watch went off with its electronic beep.

"Damn," I muttered. I didn't want the boys in the limo to think I was wearing a wire. I cradled the camcorder on my knee and bent over to shut the noise off. Just as I lowered my head I felt Mickey push me down from behind. Instantly a rapid sequence of rounds whizzed over us.

As I went flat to the ground and pulled out my automatic I heard

Mickey open fire behind me, covering me as I propped up the briefcase as a shield in front of me. I started getting off rounds into the body of the limo. I could hear Mickey continuing to fire. I looked back. She was down behind me, protected somewhat by the briefcase, the camcorder, and my body.

It looked from here like the guy in the limo was firing an Uzi submachine gun at us.

A sequence of hard shudders went through my body. I felt like I had been hit. I looked for blood. But it had only been the impact of several rounds tearing into the briefcase. I had been saved by thick cowhide and stacks of banded currency.

I started pouring rounds into the open windows until the machine-gun fire stopped. Then I shot out the other side windows and Mickey blew out the windshield and the rear window.

"Nice shooting," I yelled back to her.

With most of the glass in their car car shot away our friends in the now-customized limo had just about had enough. A few last shots rang out. By their sound, I was sure it was small weapons fire—a final gesture. The Uzi was silent. The driver put down a strip of rubber on the grass ten yards long and tore across the field in a tornado of smoke and dirt to South Drive.

I rolled over. The leather of the briefcase had been torn up by the bullets but I was okay. I was alive. Saved by Mickey and my watch alarm. I jumped up in relief.

Then I saw Mickey. She was lying on her back holding her groin while blood was gushing through her fingers.

"Oh, God," she groaned. "It hurts."

I pulled off her skirt. Her underpants were bloody. I folded up the skirt as best I could to a dry pad.

"Hold this against yourself. Hard as you can. We've got to slow the bleeding. I'm going to get some towels from the trunk."

I ran to the T-Bird and brought back two beach towels I kept back there. I took the skirt from her hands and held a folded towel up to the wound. I couldn't tell if the bleeding was slowing.

"Let's get you the hell to a hospital."

While she kept the towel pressed against the bullet wound, I carried her to the car and put her into the passenger seat as gently as I could. I was thankful that we had all stockpiled our own blood

at the city blood bank to protect us from any possibility of a transfusion with AIDS-tainted blood.

"The money and the camcorder," Mickey mumbled.

"I wasn't going to leave them. I was just taking care of you
first."

I retrieved the briefcase and the camcorder and put them back
in the trunk.

I put Mickey's leg up on the dash and gave her a new towel to
compress the wound with. I took her free hand in mine. It was like
ice.

I got the car moving.

"I'm bleeding on your precious car."

"The seats are leather. It'll wipe off."

A suggestion of a smile crossed her ashen face, which made me
feel a little better. Only a little; she had taken a bullet intended for
me.

We had come west across town on Fulton to get to the park. If I
remembered correctly, Fulton would take us all the way to Emergency Hospital. But that would still be a few miles.

I tried to break every traffic law I could to attract a cop. But no
luck. No cop in sight to escort me as I took my chances running
red lights and blowing my horn through the intersections.

At Franklin, I cut over to Grove. Emergency Hospital was on
the corner of Grove and Polk—another familiar street. I made a
right on Polk and drove up to the emergency room entrance. By
the time we reached it, Mickey had fainted. I jumped out of the car
and called for help.

Two paramedics wearing latex gloves and long-sleeved smocks
appeared and got her out of the car and on a gurney while I tried to
explain what had happened. As one strapped her down, the other
took her blood pressure. I heard the second one say, "GSW. Pupils
dilating, nonreactive. Blood pressure 100 over 70." They wheeled
her through the emergency room. As Mickey went by, the nurse
behind the desk stopped me and asked what had happened to her.

"GSW. Gunshot wound," I explained, picking up the language of
the paramedics.

"What kind?"

I didn't want to think about it. "Possibly machine gun."

The people in the waiting-room chairs looked up. We had bypassed them and what had to be their relatively minor emergencies if they could be sitting out here.

"Kind of early. We usually get the Knife-and-Gun Club people after dark on the weekends," the nurse said.

Her wiseass comment forced me to pay attention to her. She was tall and overweight and packed into a white uniform that may have fit ten years ago. Her white arms looked like giant uncooked sausage links. She had jet black hair up in a little bun that pulled the skin of her face back tight as the top of a drum. She looked like she had a good facelift malpractice case.

I wanted to know what was going on with Mickey but all she wanted to know about was medical insurance. I informed her about Mickey's own blood stored at the blood bank.

"Was she expecting to be shot?"

"It happens in our line of work."

"What are you, dope dealers?"

I restrained myself. "Private detectives," I said.

Her look told me that was just as bad. But I did have our group card and medical number, which raised our status and made her very happy. I spent a half hour filling out the appropriate forms for the uptight lady in white. When other patients tried to get her attention, she disappeared.

"Could you tell me what's happening?" I asked her when she finally returned.

She smiled. "Take a seat while I go over these papers," she said, taking the forms I had filled out.

"Is she being operated on?" I asked.

"I don't know. I'm out here with you. And there are other people to attend to."

I thought about asking her if I could use her phone but I knew she would only point out the pay phones at the back of the room.

Out of courtesy and out of hope that he would get some respect in this hospital, I called Glenn, who showed up twenty minutes later. He had managed to hitch a ride on an ambulance going to Emergency. By the time he arrived, I still hadn't learned anything.

Dr. Earnhard demanded to know everything now. He wanted the name of the doctor. He demanded to be admitted to the operating room. He wanted to see Mickey's chart. He wanted to see Mickey. In general, he got on the nerves of the admitting nurse much more than I. All of her suppressed hostility toward doctors rushed out of her toward him like a hurricane.

She let Dr. Earnhard know exactly where he stood in this hospital. Nowhere. She told him he had no rights or privileges in Emergency Hospital and if he didn't shut the hell up, she was going to call the orderlies and have him removed.

"Damn you," he shouted. "Do you know who I am?"

"Or would you rather have me call the police?" Apparently, she'd never caught his act on TV.

"I'll have your job, nurse."

"You can take it and shove it!"

Glenn looked at me. He knew there was nothing to do but give up, just as I had done.

"The union has made them all insufferable bitches," he muttered to me.

We both sat down. While we waited I described exactly what had happened, how I had treated the wound, and how long it had taken me to drive her here.

When I finished, he asked in a tightly controlled voice, "How could you let her be out there?"

"She wanted to be. That's her job. I don't feel very good about it, but she saved my life."

He didn't answer. It was a sure bet he didn't think much of the trade.

Finally, a small man, with dark skin and curly black hair, emerged, asking for me. He wore a green smock and cap. His surgeon's mask hung loose about his neck. He identified himself as Dr. Thornday, the surgeon attending Mickey. He spoke with a lilting accent I couldn't quite place.

I introduced Glenn as Dr. Earnhard, a family friend.

Without missing a beat, Dr. Thornday gave us the specifics. He hadn't caught Glenn's act, either. "The lady was hit in the groin, close to the joint with the thigh. The bullet was not deflected by bone. It passed cleanly by her lower intestine, her reproductive organs, and bladder, into her left buttock where it lodged. We removed the bullet and closed the wound. Luckily it was of small caliber. A GSW from a machine gun would be quite a different thing. We would be looking at a war wound, the kind of thing once seen only in combat, but all too common in our cities these days."

One of those last shots had hit her, I thought. But at least it hadn't been a round from the Uzi.

"Did she need a transfusion?" Glenn asked.

"Yes. One was required. Her own blood was delivered."

"We keep a supply at the blood bank. Just in case," I explained to Glenn.

"What is the prognosis?" he asked the surgeon.

"It is excellent. She is a very lucky lady. As a doctor, you know what damage could have been done."

"I don't want to think about it," he said.

Neither did I.

"I'd like to see her," Glenn said.

"So would I."

"Give her another half hour. She is still coming out of it. And one at a time. She's in recovery room four, basement level.

We sat down again. Thirty minutes flew like hours. I let Glenn go first.

After fifteen minutes, he came out and said, "Damn woman!"

"What do you mean?" I asked as I got up.

"None of your business," he said and pushed past me toward the exit.

"Hey!"

He stopped and turned. "Don't forget tennis on Wednesday."

I had forgotten all about it. It hardly seemed important at the moment but I said, "How could I?"

"Good." He went out the exit door.

As I went past the nurse at the desk, I smiled at her. She didn't smile back. Mickey was lying flat on her stomach with an IV suspended over her. I could only see the left side of her face, which was as white as the hospital pillowcase.

I sat down by the head of the bed so she could talk to me without moving.

"That charming doctor told me how lucky I was."

"Which one, Earnhard or Thornday?"

"The one with the musical accent."

"He sounded like he knew what he was doing."

"Let's hope so. He told me nothing important was hit." She tried to point at herself under the thin sheet but gave up.

"Depends on what he thinks is important."

She laughed. "Don't make me laugh. It hurts."

Considering the situation, she was in pretty good spirits.

"Did they give you pain pills?" I asked.

"I've screamed for them already."

"And they're coming," a young nurse who had just entered the room said. She gave Mickey two pills and held a straw in a cup of water so Mickey could drink without raising her head. "They'll start working shortly," she said and left.

"Thank God," Mickey said.

I gave her a hug and held her for a long time. I kissed her cheek. "You saved my life," I said.

"You owe me, Jeremiah," she said with a half yawn. "Those pain pills work fast. I feel sleepy already."

"Don't fight it," I said. I kissed the back of her head and added "I do owe you" as I left.

Driving back, I went over what had happened. Obviously, I had been set up. What pissed me off was that I should have picked up on it.

Starborn could have been a dupe or just as easily could have set the whole thing up. But why? For the same reason as the break-in which took place right after Starborn had a chance to case my office. He was tied—as Siamese twin—to Bloodhart and we were getting too close to the general and his operation.

Well, I was going to have to get a hell of a lot closer to the Church of the Second Coming—Western Rite.

I went outside with a bucket of water and a sponge and rinsed the Pacific salt from the exterior of the car and Mickey's blood from the leather bench seat. I squeezed the sponge over the gutter and watched the primal fluids flow pink and foaming to the sewer. I shivered in the warm sunshine.

21

I drove up to Mendocino County the next morning to give something back to Reverend Starborn. But before visiting his church complex, I stopped at the county center. I found the Tax Collector's Office and got into the real estate property records, which like most documents in California—including death certificates—are public information. I learned some interesting things about land ownership and the Starborn operation.

I drove on to the church and parked in a vast lot that surrounded a huge concrete structure that reminded me of a Frenchman's beret—except for the cross rising to the heavens at its peak. I got the bullet-torn briefcase out of the trunk, went through two ornately carved doors and into the Church of the Second Coming—Western Rite. Its auditorium, full of plush theater seats, cameras, booms, and spotlights, looked more like a TV studio than a cathedral. But the huge rose window in gold and white that took up most of the back wall was impressive enough to lend an air of ecclesiastical respectability—almost. There was a gold-plated pulpit.

"Can I help you, sir?" a voice asked politely. "I'm Deacon Rollins."

I turned and saw a young man who looked like a steroid-fed

weightlifter wearing a black suit and a brush cut. I didn't see how
the seams of the suit stayed intact.

"I'm looking for Reverend Starborn."

"Do you have an appointment?" he asked even more politely. If
this guy was supposed to be a bodyguard, he was the politest one I
had ever run into.

"No. Do I need one?"

"Usually."

"Could you take him a message?"

"Certainly."

He led me to an actual wooden pew—one of two in the front of
the studio-church—and I sat down. I imagined the cameras spent
a lot of time focused right here.

"What is your message?"

"Tell the Reverend: St. John lives."

"Is that the Baptist or the Evangelist?"

"Neither one. The P.I. With something to return to him."

The Deacon left me. Maybe he wasn't a bodyguard after all. Just
an extra-large born-again Christian.

He returned in less than five minutes and led me behind the
gold-plated pulpit and choir risers through a massive golden curtain to what in most churches would be the sanctuary. In this
church, it was a dressing-room area. We stopped in front of a door
with Starborn's name on it. I was glad to see that there was a cruci-
fix not a star on his door.

The Deacon held the door open for me. The reverend was in his
customary white. Like his church, everything in the room was furnished in shades of gold. The only odd piece was a black leather
couch that stood under a small stained-glass window depicting a
golden-haired Christ crushing Satan.

I nodded to Starborn and gestured toward the deacon. "Is he
staying?" I asked as I dropped the briefcase on the table in front of
the couch.

Starborn dismissed him with a wave of his hand. The huge deacon was not a confidant.

With the door closed behind us, I said, "You set me up."

"I don't know what you're talking about."

"When my partner and I got there, these blackmailers opened
fire."

"But you're okay."

"My partner's in the hospital."

"I'm sorry."

"You were so interested in the outcome that you didn't bother to call to find out if I had the tapes of your wife."

"I was waiting for your call . . ."

"You thought I was dead." I moved toward him.

"Get back. Or I'll call for Deacon Rollins."

"I wouldn't do that." I grabbed the reverend and put an arm lock on his neck. Hard to call anybody.

"I don't know what you're talking about," he choked out.

"Oh, no?" I increased my pressure and his pain. "You didn't know about the reception planned for me? Complete with a welcoming machine-gun salute?"

"I'm telling you . . ." The guy was tougher than I expected. So I hurt him more.

"What are you telling me?"

"I didn't know it was a trap."

"Bullshit, Reverend."

"Rollins! he managed to get out. Not loud enough for the deacon to hear unless he had his ear to the door. No such luck for Starborn. I cut off his windpipe and pulled out my gun.

"You're choking me! Please!"

"No Rollins."

"Okay. Okay. Stop choking me. You were set up."

"Now that's better. By whom?" I loosened my hold.

"I don't know."

"That's not better. You don't want to lie in church," I said as I rubbed the cold barrel of the gun along his temple. "Who was it?" I demanded.

The reverend coughed up the name Bloodhart. "He sent me to you."

"You set up the break-in?"

"Yes. That's why I went to your office."

"You're his partner, aren't you? His Siamese twin."

"What?"

"You're working together." I let him sit down and put away my gun.

"In a manner of speaking."

"Explain."

"We use the money we raised through the Church to help his cause."

"What cause?"

"Fighting the yellow peril at home and overseas."

"But Bloodhart got impatient with raising money your way for the cause. Through the voluntary contributions of the gullible."

"Yes. It was never enough. And of course a substantial amount had to go back into the church operation. We were always arguing about that."

"So he went into extortion and a protection racket that preyed on the Vietnamese he hated."

"I didn't have any part in that," Starborn insisted. "I am a man of God."

"Did Bloodhart have Vincent Gutman killed?"

"I don't know anything about that."

I pushed the gun into his temple. "Try to think of something."

"Bloodhart told me he had nothing to do with it."

"I'm supposed to believe that?" I asked.

"I swear to God. An oath I do not take lightly. That is what he said."

"Why did you get involved in setting me up?"

He hesitated.

"Come on. Make it easy on yourself."

"That deal for the tapes? Bloodhart has them of my wife."

"That wasn't a scam?"

"No. He ... uses them ... to get me to go along with him."

"Where is he?"

"I don't know."

"How many men does he have with him?"

"I don't know."

"I know the Church owns a boy's camp up by Black Lake. Is that where they are?"

"Yes."

"Do you have a map of the area?" I tapped his head with the barrel.

"Yes." He got out a detailed county map and showed me the dirt road that led into the hills and the camp. "There are no signs," he said.

"I'll find it." I folded up the map. "I appreciate your help. I'll see what I can do about the tapes," I said.

He looked stunned. Then he brushed himself off, acting like we had been wrestling on the floor.

"Are you serious?"

"Yes."

"Why?" he asked.

"Oh, it won't be for free." I pointed to the briefcase containing the $25,000.

"That's outrageous."

"Not if you're telling me the truth," I said. "What is your wife worth to you?"

He dropped his eyes.

I gestured at the briefcase. "Don't go and blow it." I didn't ask whose money it really was. I didn't give a damn.

"You are serious."

"I don't much like blackmail. Even if somebody's taking a guy like you. Besides your wife looks like a nice lady." I grinned at him. "And the agency could use the money." Collecting that would make me a hero to my partners. Then I added, "It's also an incentive to keep you quiet. I wouldn't want the general to hear about my visit."

I followed the county road indicated on the map—not recommended for trucks and trailers—until I came to the dirt road turn-off that led to Black Lake Camp. There was no sign, just like the Reverend had said. I estimated that it was seven miles to the lake and figured I could drive in about five before hiking the rest of the way in. But I was wrong. The road got so bad, I had to abandon my car after about three miles. I parked it behind some rocks and shrubbery. I put on my running shoes and started hiking. I hoped I wouldn't run into a Bloodhart patrol.

The only things I ran into were deer and rabbits. I spotted a few marijuana fields and gave them a wide berth. Almost certainly they were all booby-trapped. I stayed as close as I could to the dirt road. It was hot and the terrain was steep. I was glad I'd brought a canteen along.

The four miles took me nearly an hour and a half to cover. A small lake was spread out below me. I could see thick patches of lake weed growing from its bottom. On its western edge was a camp that had been turned into a quasi-army base. Men in fatigues moved about the barracks. Barbed wire rolled in a continuous coil around the perimeter. Men carrying what looked like AK-47's walked along its length. A few makeshift guardhouses were set up at various points. I almost cried out when I saw the Chief at the north end of one of the guardhouses. He moved along the northern perimeter on patrol. He was dressed in army fatigues and carried the same weapon as the others.

I swung over in his direction and came down a slope, moving beneath the thick vegetation. His patrol done, the Chief was sitting in the shade inside the guardhouse. I tossed some rocks his way.

He came out with his AK-47 at the ready.

"It's me," I whispered from behind a rock. I stuck my head up.

"Jeremiah! It is about time that you got here."

I ducked back down. He sat on top of the rock.

"What the hell is this place?"

"A prison. We have a warden. We have guards. And we have trustees who get out on leaves. They do the extortion work on the outside."

"What have you found out?

The Chief stretched back, getting closer to me. "Gutman was here. But he was not into Bloodhart's extortion program. He escaped to go out on his own personal warpath."

"Maybe Bloodhart found him," I said.

"I have heard nothing about that," Chief Moses said.

"How does Bloodhart keep all of this from the government?"

Chief Moses laughed softy. "He doesn't. This is a top-secret debriefing camp for returning MIA's. There's covert CIA backing. Bloodhart's got an arsenal here of weapons diverted from shipments going to Israel and other allies."

"You've learned a lot."

"Some men love to talk. I prefer to listen."

"But don't these guys want out?"

"Some do. Like Gutman. A lot seem brainwashed. Some are blackmailed with the threat of charges of collaboration or massacres like My Lai Village. Some are afraid to go back to the world. They have been prisoners too long. But Bloodhart also makes the big crusade pitch that gets most of them. They are preparing for one last battle to save the West and their buddies in Vietnam from the yellow terror. He has pinpointed a prison on the outskirts of Hanoi where, he claims, all known POW's are being held. After this military operation, the men have been promised $10,000 each—from the CIA."

"This is a movie fantasy," I said.

"It is working. And of course he cannot write off the war. So we are about to invade Vietnam."

"Unbelievable. When?"

"Bloodhart will be out here Thursday. He comes in by his own personal helicopter, which he pilots himself. We are scheduled to leave on Friday." He pointed to the olive-green trucks parked at the south end of the base. A real convoy.

"Now that you are here, do you have a plan?" he asked.

"We're going to put one together right now," I said.

The plan called for an assault on the camp on Thursday when Bloodhart would be there.

"It will take an army," he said.

"I can arrange that." I hoped I could. "Don't worry."

"Me worry? When everything is in your capable hands?"

"Right."

"White man, I do not wish to find myself on a transport to Vietnam."

"Just give me the signal on Thursday and we'll take this camp."

"Look for a smoke signal."

"What do you mean?"

He pointed to a square concrete building in the center of the camp. "It is the arsenal."

"And when it goes up in smoke..."

"Send in your braves," he said.

One of the vets was moving in our direction. The Chief stood up and waved his arm back and forth.

"Everything okay, Mosby?" the other man called.

"Okay," the Chief called back. "Just a deer."

The other man paused and then did a slow about-face. It was time for me to get the hell out of there.

I hiked back up the hill to the road and then walked to the car. I drove back on the dirt road. Dust coated my throat and I was long out of water. I was dying for a beer. Any kind. Even from a can.

Back in San Francisco, I went about doing what I had promised Chief Moses. I went out to raise an army of my own.

I drove over to the Dragon Seeds and cornered Curtis. "Man, I need your help."

"This another grocery store stakeout?" he asked.

"Not exactly. This is more like war," I explained. It didn't much appeal to Curtis.

"We've got to get these vets away from him. Or they'll all end up dead."

"Where we get the weapons for this war?"

"I'll take care of it."

"Afraid you'd say that." He told me to wait in in the back room while he talked to the men out front. I could hear them arguing and I could hear Curtis persuading. When Curtis threw the door open and said, "The Dragon Seeds are with you, man," I let out a yell.

I went out to my car. Hubcaps still there; everything else intact. The Tenderloin was becoming downright safe. I drove a few streets over to Little Saigon and found a parking space a half block from the Yellow Suns Social and Athletic Club.

I hadn't been in the building in a while. I was surprised at all of the bodybuilding equipment and the walls lined with mirrors. The room was full of young Vietnamese men working out and admiring themselves in the mirrors.

In the center of the gym was a boxing ring and around that a number of speed bags and body punching bags. In the ring two kids who looked about sixteen were slugging it out. A heavy middle-aged man was trying to referee the bout without much success. Every fifth or sixth punch landed on him.

I found Tram Van Dam in a private back room wearing a Gold's Gym sweatshirt. As usual, his head was shaved and he sported a mustache and goatee. But he seemed to have gained about fifty pounds of solid muscle. I suspected steroids.

"You've grown."

"Hard work in the gym." A trace of an accent that he had struggled to get rid of remained. He looked at me with suspicion. "Why are you here?"

"I need some help." I laid out what I needed in weapons from the Yellow Suns.

"Why do you need these AK-47's? This is no P.I. work."

I explained about Bloodhart and the Dragon Seeds. "Can you supply them?"

"Yes," he said and grinned. "For such a cause."

"Good," I said.

"Why do you not use Vietnamese men?"

It took me a moment to understand. "You want to go out there?"

"Of course. Some things are business and some things are pleasure. Would not miss this for a million dollars."

That was fine with me. I had the weapons lined up and I had just about doubled the size of my ragtag United Nations army.

I headed back to my office satisfied with myself. I was in command of fifteen Vietnam vets and a dozen Vietnamese gang members, all of whom were going to be armed with AK-47 automatic assault rifles.

General St. John. I liked the way it sounded. I smiled foolishly at myself in the rearview mirror.

I stopped in to visit Mickey that night just in time to bump into Glenn leaving her room. He didn't look any happier than he did the previous day when he left.

"What's bothering Glenn," I asked.

"It's personal."

I didn't push it.

"With you lying here, playing tennis over you doesn't seem the right thing to do." I said to Mickey, who was recovering and could now rest in bed on her side. Color had returned to her face.

"Please go ahead. Don't ask so many questions. Just go ahead." She tried to sit up straight in bed to punctuate her point. "Ow! That still hurts." She rolled back on her elbow. "But do what I say, anyway."

"At your service," I said.

On Wednesday, at the Yellow Suns Club, I went over the details of the battle plan with Curtis and Tram Van Dam using Starborn's map and a diagram I did of the camp layout from memory. We were in the back room, surrounded by crates of automatic weapons. The vets and Vietnamese were out in the gym. I hoped the Vietnam War wouldn't be refought.

Tram Van Dam had changed his style since yesterday. He wore a dark green three-piece suit that made him look like a Pacific Rim businessman. Curtis was dressed as usual. Both of the men chainsmoked.

When we came out, the men were fooling around with the weights and punching bags and medicine balls. My army was getting along.

We split the men up and sent them to every vehicle rental agency in the city. By the afternoon, we had all of the four-wheel-drive trucks we needed to move our army of thirty. We put in supplies, which meant automatic weapons and hundreds of rounds. But mostly we put in sandwiches and cases of beer. This was going to be a very short war if everything went as planned.

Next stop was to break up the convoy. Each truck was driven to a different parking garage or lot in the area. The troops were divided into groups of three with one man as driver. At 0800 each of the ten trucks would be picked up. That would carry the thirty of us up 101 to the Mendicino County border, where we would regroup before heading for Black Lake Camp.

With everything in place, I was ready to play tennis with Glenn. I changed into a purple and gold San Francisco State Tennis T-shirt and shorts that almost matched. I drove over to Glenn's club and found him in glaring tennis whites outside on the first court doing stretching exercises under the lights. I started the same routine, working from my Achilles tendons and hamstrings up to my neck muscles. Getting limber for the showdown.

And it was a showdown. He took the first set 7–5, to the loud applause of a crowd that had gathered in a small grandstand by the court.

Their reaction, along with the image of Mickey, inspired me in the second set. I held service and turned around the score to 7–5 in my favor. For the third set, he broke out a new can of balls.

We stayed so even, we ended up in a tiebreaker to settle the match. The crowd was applauding his points and silent at mine. I though of Mickey in a tennis dress. That got me a backhand winner down the line on a service return. And a match point, which I promptly blew with a double fault.

Glenn called my forehand out when I could see that it was clearly inside the line. He threw his fist up to the lights and the stars. His club applauded. I was pissed off. He had a match point.

He followed his serve to the net and I returned it right at his stomach. It made a dull plop when it hit. The crowd of about thirty gave a collective gasp. The doctor was bent over. His toupee had slipped forward on his forehead. He gradually unbent, straightened his hair and glared at me.

"I guess that one landed in," I yelled across the net.

He didn't say a word.

This time he served without charging the net. I hit the return toward the middle of the court where he couldn't cheat me. I kept the ball well inside the lines and to his backhand. My patience paid off. He made an unforced error that infuriated him. I had match point again and the serve. I faulted. My second serve went deep but he hit a good return. I hit my backhand too low and the ball struck the tape on top of the net. A loser. But instead of dropping on my side, it rolled along the tape for about a foot, and then dropped. On his side. The match was mine on a lucky shot.

"Sorry," I said, following proper tennis club etiquette for net-ball winners.

"Fuck off," he said as he came forward to offer me the customary handshake. Somehow, I didn't think his heart was in the gesture.

Most of the people in the grandstand applauded politely. They weren't such a bad bunch after all.

I had a beer at the bar, which I put on Glenn's tab, and then showered in the locker room.

I drove to Emergency and parked in the lot for visitors. It was after hours but I had a lab coat from our supply of office disguises and put it on in the car. No one stopped me at the entrance or from riding the elevator up to the third floor.

I made my way to Mickey's private room and slipped inside. The hospital obviously had to do something about security.

Mickey was lying on her side in bed, watching TV on the wall in front of her.

I closed the door behind me and I snuck right into Mickey's bed beside her.

"Jeremiah," she whispered, "what are you doing?"

"I won."

"I deduced that. But I repeat. What the hell are you doing?"

We were playing a game. I had no illusions that Mickey would drop Glenn for me because I had won a tennis match.

"Collecting. Getting into a hospital bed with a beautiful woman has always been a fantasy of mine."

She was quiet for several moments. "You want to know why Glenn was upset yesterday?"

"I was curious."

"Glenn and I broke up."

"Why?"

"He issued me an ultimatum. I quit the P.I. business or it's all over between us."

I propped myself up on an elbow and admired Mickey. "And you said no."

"Damn right. He wants me to sit at home and have a brood of his babies."

"That's not so bad."

"But I'm not ready for that, Jeremiah."

"I don't know about that," I said.

"Don't you start, too."

"You almost got killed."

"But I didn't. So don't—"

I hugged her into silence.

Finally she whispered, "Get out of here before a nurse comes in."

I got out of her bed and made my escape.

22

By 1100 hours Thursday morning, we were a convoy massed at the Mendocino County border. We continued north on 101 until we turned off onto the same winding country road I had taken two days ago. The trucks we rented were small enough to maneuver the hairpin turns. On the unmarked dirt road to Bloodhart's camp, we shifted into four-wheel drive.

As we moved, our vehicles raised a cloud of dry dust that might be visible at the lake. I called for a halt a mile away from the camp. From there we hiked with our weapons, backpacks, and the grumblings of the troops, who hadn't signed on for a forced march.

Ignoring my warning about booby traps, some of the soldiers wandered off into the marijuana fields to cut themselves some pot. One of them barely escaped being cut by a knife released by a trip wire. One almost set off a shotgun trap that would have blown off his head and alerted the camp, and one barely escaped from a Doberman that had been left behind to guard a field of plants like a junkyard dog. From then on, excursions into the mined pot fields lost their attraction.

When we got close enough to see the camp, I stopped the march and we scattered among the rocks. We waited. Apparently, we hadn't been spotted.

As 1300 hours approached, I watched for the smoke signals the

Chief had promised. Smoke signals was a nice euphemism for blowing up Bloodhart's arsenal. The concrete structure looked formidable. He didn't let us down. At 1300 hours exactly, its wooden roof went up in flames and a minute later there was an explosion and one of the concrete walls collapsed. During the confusion, the Chief appeared at the gate in the barbed wire, opened it, and joined us.

"How'd you do it, Chief?" I asked.

"Flaming arrows, white man."

"What are we up against in firepower?"

"Little. Ammunition and most weapons were stored in the arsenal. Only the guards carried weapons."

Our army poured in brandishing AK-47's, which were not to be fired except in a life-threatening situation. It wasn't much of a battle. As the Chief indicated, most of Bloodhart's soldiers didn't have weapons. A few shots were fired but even those who were armed were ready to surrender. They all looked stunned by my army of Vietnamese and Americans and our thirty AK-47's. In fifteen minutes, we had almost all of the weapons that didn't go up in flames in our hands.

The only resistance remaining was coming from a large wooden building with a porch and supporting pillars that looked like it had been the camp lodge.

I left Curtis and Van Dam to herd the prisoners into a single barracks and set up a guard. The Chief and I moved closer to the lodge, using the trees for cover. Several rounds flew over our heads from a knocked-out window.

"That is Bloodhart's headquarters. He had an AK-47 in there. And there is a helicopter under all that foliage behind it."

Several more rounds came tearing out of the window. We didn't return the fire. We just moved forward and waited.

Several minutes passed and then a man appeared on the porch brandishing his weapon. He was hatless, but dressed in some kind of formal uniform. He looked like a barrel of a man under a short blond crewcut.

"That is him," Chief Moses said.

"Where'd you find this goddamn gook army!" the general yelled. He opened fire and stepped back into the lodge.

The Chief and I went flat to the ground. The rounds tore up a seam of earth between us.

Bloodhart continued to spray rounds from the window and we couldn't lift our heads.

Suddenly he stopped. We moved to better cover behind some redwood trees. We listened and waited for him to start firing again. When he didn't, we began to move cautiously toward the porch of the building.

From the porch, we heard the chopper behind the lodge whir into life. We started running toward the back of the lodge but as we came around the corner the chopper lifted up. He was getting away. But Bloodhart had not had time to remove all of the camouflage. The rear rotors were tangled with ropes and vegetation. The chopper rose higher, hovered, strained like a living beast, and then, at the moment it was about to break free, the rear blades began to shatter. It was losing its stability. First it rocked violently from side to side, and then it seemed to right itself. The main rotor above the roof whined and the helicopter flipped over in midair like a wounded duck. In the next few seconds, it came down in a grove of redwoods and went up in flames as quickly as the arsenal had.

We rushed to the crash site, where Bloodhart was trying to get out of the chopper door behind a solid wall of flames. I moved forward, thinking I could help get him out, while the Chief yelled for me to get back. When I didn't, he tackled me from behind just as the fuel tank exploded and the chopper turned into a fireball.

General Bloodhart had fought his last battle.

Everyone came out of the barracks to watch the blaze. It marked the end of everything. There were no more prisoners and guards, Vietnamese and Americans. Just men who had shared another moment of war. I imagined Christopher Cook was among them. Our men passed out cigarettes and they all started to talk to each other, identifying outfits and units and zones. It was if we had entered a POW camp and freed the prisoners.

I recognized Richard Martini and he came over and shook my hand.

"Bloodhart wasn't crazy," he said. But ..."

"He's dead."

One of Bloodhart's men, a short thin guy with a scraggly beard, came up to me and said, "I'm speakin' for all of us. Take us home, man. We been away from the world too long."

We led the men back to the trucks. Their spirits improved the farther we got away from the camp. We got out sandwiches and beer and had a welcome home party and a wake for Bloodhart. Some of the men made sentimental speeches about the dead general but most of them ate and drank in silence.

I remembered something. "Chief. Take charge. I've got to go back."

I drove one of the trucks back to the lodge. I was looking for two things. Some kind of clue to tie Bloodhart to Gutman's murder and the videotapes he had of Starborn's wife.

The lodge had been converted into a general's headquarters, complete with pictures of Douglas MacArthur, Ulysses Grant, and George Patton. There was an American flag and a large wooden desk in the center of the open room. Against one wall were five wooden filing cabinets. There were records, names, dates, all kinds of information on MIA's that the army could use. The file on Gutman listed him as AWOL and that was it. Except for the TV and VCR sitting on a table in front of the desk. There was a tape in it and I pushed the play button.

George C. Scott appeared in front of a huge American flag. I ejected the tape. Under the table there was a box of videotapes, most of them war films. But three tapes were only marked with the letter S. I put one of these into the VCR and started it.

A naked young man I didn't recognize came on the screen and then a naked woman I did recognize. I let it run for a few minutes to make sure I had the right lady. Reverend Starborn was right. She was memorable. I rewound the tape and put it into a pocket of my fatigues. I checked the other two, fast-forwarding to Mrs. Starborn.

I got back to the trucks as the party was winding down. The mood was upbeat as we all headed south for the city. We got there by nine o'clock and deposited Bloodhart's MIA army at the circle in front of Letterman. Curtis and Tram Van Dam wanted no part of the red tape and no questions about the weapons in the trucks. I let them all drive off.

The Chief and I led the vets into the Letterman lobby. The staff couldn't believe it. Dr. Koyota couldn't believe it, but he loved it.

More publicity for the man. I refused to answer any questions, except to identify the site of the camp. Koyota threatened to call the MP's and the CIA but we escaped before he could follow through on it. We returned our truck to the rental agency without a single bullet hole in it. And picked up my T-Bird.

On the way to the Chief's I told him what had happened to Mickey when we had gone to make the exchange for Starborn.

"Why did you not tell me before?"

"I didn't want to upset you. You had delicate work to do at the camp."

Chief Moses grunted. "I want to see her."

"It's too late."

"Now!"

We stopped at the office and got lab coats. We got into Mickey's room without any trouble. Security had not improved.

When she opened her eyes and saw both of us, she grinned and said, "Don't tell me the Chief beat Glenn at tennis, too."

"No such luck," I said.

"What is the squaw talking about?" Chief Moses asked.

"Just give this woman a hug, Chief," I said.

That was exactly what he did.

23

Sunday night we were trying to celebrate. The Chief had survived
boot camp; Mickey was out of the hospital; and I was almost satisfied with how the case had turned out.

We were sitting, Mickey on a special cushion, at the Hyde Street
Grille having dinner. We stuck with the Pakistani specials and with
Bud, white wine, and Henry's. Familiarity made things seem nor-
mal again.

"You are not satisfied, are you, Jeremiah?" Chief Moses asked.

"No," I admitted. "There was no real evidence to tie Gutman's
death to Bloodhart."

"But we've put everything together," Mickey said.

"Only if we go along with the police line that Gutman killed his
own daughter. But there isn't a shred of evidence that he was actually out there."

"Then who is the killer?" the Chief asked.

"A copycat."

"Who?" Mickey asked.

"Let's back it up. Assume it was a copycat. Who was Jackie
meeting?"

"A customer to blackmail," Chief Moses said.

"Or the copycat to blackmail."

"What did she have on him?" Mickey asked.

"I have a hunch. Mickey, remember how the little girl reacted to your play?"

"How could I ever forget?"

"What are you talking about?" the Chief asked.

Mickey told him about the case his work for the Archbishop had brought us.

"Go on," he said to me after she finished.

"The little girl wrote that note because she was ashamed to say anything at first."

"So?" Mickey asked.

"Jackie left a note she wanted her father to have."

"You can't equate a prostitute with a scared child," she said.

"I do not agree. Jeremiah may be on to something," the Chief said.

"We need some evidence," Mickey said.

I ordered another round of drinks. "You have a contact in the phone company," I said to Mickey. "Use him. Remember how Gutman didn't have a phone in his motel room so we assumed he didn't make any calls we could trace. There are at least three pay phones a block in either direction. Get a record of the calls made on those phones on Saturday the seventh and Sunday the eighth."

She shifted uncomfortably in her chair. "I'm really starting to hurt."

"I'll drive you home right now. You can call your contact in the morning."

"I'm going to owe this guy," Mickey said.

"Don't worry. He'll need us someday."

"I hope so. Can we go now?"

We did.

On Monday my watch alarm went off, reminding me that it had helped save my life and that I had to move my car. Not a bad combination.

Mickey called to say that she was in too much pain to come in that morning but she would try to get the information we needed from the phone company. Mid-afternoon, she arrived by cab with the printout of all the calls made from the pay phones on those two blocks. The Chief, Mickey, and I scanned it. It took us only five minutes to find the area code and number my hunch told me would be there.

"Look at this number and look at the time of day the call was made. Just about right to get the call, drive into the city, and do the job. Chief, let's take a ride. Mickey, I don't think you ought to chance it."

"I don't care how much it hurts, I'm going, " Mickey said.

The traffic moved almost imperceptibly out of the city on the Oakland Bay Bridge. We were in the middle of rush hour gridlock. Which gave us plenty of time to plan our approach. We decided to use the Chief. I had a Pacific Gas and Electric card in the glove compartment and I gave it to him. Chief Moses would say that there was a gas leak in the house and it had to be evacuated for at least an hour while he fixed it. That would give us the time we needed to go through the house.

It took us two hours to cover the fifty miles. Mickey didn't complain but I knew she was very uncomfortable.

When we got there, the place was empty. The gas leak plan now became an emergency backup—to be used if the occupants showed up. We left the Chief in front of the house ready with his PG&E card while I went back to the basics. It was a cinch to pick the lock and get inside. The house was now fully furnished.

"What if we don't find the letter?" Mickey asked.

"We look for a memento. Some kind of evidence."

We went into the room that was set up as a study. This letter would be locked up. I popped open a strong box and found a collection of birth certificates and insurance policies. But not the letter. A second box was full of more of the kinds of papers our society generates. But this one also had a lot of personal things. Like old love letters. Under a will, I found a brown sealed envelope. It didn't contain the letter I was looking for but instead three Polaroid pictures of a young girl definitely not dressed for choir practice.

I showed them to Mickey.

"Son of a bitch," Mickey said. "That's bondage. Is that her?"

I nodded. I went out in front and got the Chief. I showed him what we had found.

"No more games," I said. "Now we just wait."

We went into the living room and sat down on the new furniture and waited for the owners to arrive.

About an hour later, we were sitting in the dark when we heard a car pull up. A few minutes later, the front door opened and Clyde Shatts put on the living room light. Barbara followed him in.

They looked at the three of us. "What the hell are you doing here?" Clyde shouted as he slammed the door behind him.

I stood up. "You've got a problem."

"No. You do. I'm calling the police."

"I wouldn't do that just yet," I said.

The Chief moved toward Clyde to reinforce my point. Mickey, still in pain, stayed seated.

"Vincent Gutman called here the morning he was killed," I said.

"That's a lie," Clyde said.

"We have the phone records," Mickey said.

"Who spoke to him?" the Chief asked.

There was a long silence.

"I did," Barbara said shakily.

Clyde glared at her.

"What did he want?" I asked.

Clyde moved closer to the gun case by the fireplace. So did Chief Moses.

"He said he had to see me. That he had to show me something from Jackie."

"Did you go?"

She shook her head. "No. I told Clyde. He went."

"Why?" Mickey asked her.

"I was afraid."

I looked at Clyde. "You went to see him on Sunday and he wound up dead."

"Gutman was dead when I got there," Clyde yelled.

"That's what he told me," Barbara said.

Hardly reliable information. "Where's the letter?" I asked.

"What letter?"

"The letter Vincent had from his daughter. The one she took such pains to get to him."

"I don't know what you're talking about. He was dead when I got there!" Clyde was near hysteria.

"The letter about these and what you did to her..." I tossed the pictures on the new coffee table and turned to Barbara, who picked them up.

"Oh, my God! She's just a child."

"Vincent was going to tell you all about Clyde and Jackie."

"That's crazy," Clyde screamed.

"That's why you killed him, Clyde," Mickey said.

"I didn't. I said..."

"Barbara, where was Clyde the day that Jackie was murdered in Nevada?" I asked.

"At a teacher's convention in Reno."

"Convenient," the Chief said.

"Jackie was trying to blackmail you, Clyde. She had stayed in touch with her mother and she knew about the money you had inherited. This was her chance. It was the money or your career. You wanted them both. So you killed her to shut her up. And when Gutman got her letter, he was next."

"You don't have any proof," Clyde said coldly.

"Did she tell you that she had sent that letter to Gutman before she died?" I asked.

Clyde said nothing.

"It became obvious to me when I realized the copycat killer had to know that Jackie was Gutman's daughter. Otherwise imitating the April Fool Killer made no sense. You were one of the few to know. But she had sent that letter to complete her revenge. Your money and your career. When Gutman found out about your incestuous relationship, he was going to give the letter to Barbara. That's why you killed him."

He moved toward the guns near the mantel but the Chief stopped him.

"We have a witness who can place your brown Datsun at the vista point where Jackie was murdered." It was a leap of faith from the dirty foreign car Sherry recalled but it got us through the bull.

"I want a lawyer," he shouted.

"You only get one call. Read him his rights, Chief," I said.

Suddenly Mickey cried out, trying to get up as Barbara put her fist through the glass gun case and grabbed a Colt .45 before anyone could stop her.

She pointed the gun at Clyde. The ivory handle was dripping with blood from her cut hand.

"No," I called out. It was the gun Clyde kept loaded.

The Chief pushed Clyde across the room away from his wife.

It didn't do much good. Barbara fired twice. Clyde spun around like a drunken dancer and went down on the new carpeting. In a moment there was a pool of blood under him.

I moved toward Barbara and she said, "Get back. He's still alive."

She was waving the bloody Colt in the air.

"It's over," Mickey said.

"Put it down," I said.

Barbara collapsed into a chair. She let the gun fall to the carpet. She was sobbing.

The Chief dialed 911 for an ambulance.

"I could sense what was going on with Clyde and Jackie. That's why I was relieved when she ran away. But I couldn't admit it to myself." She picked up the Polaroids and threw them disgustedly at Clyde.

"Please," Clyde pleaded. "I'm sorry."

"What about Jessica?" she asked.

Clyde just shook his head.

"Thank God Jessica isn't here tonight," Barbara whispered between sobs.

I went to get a towel and ice for her bleeding hand. The siren of an ambulance racing through the suburbs pierced the room.

24

On the last Friday in May, four days after Barbara Shatts shot her husband, Mickey, the Chief, and I were having a small celebration at her apartment on the Embarcadero where the view of the Oakland Bay Bridge was spectacular.

Mickey was celebrating being on the mend, I was belatedly celebrating my birthday, and the Chief was celebrating life in general. Their gift to me was a case of Wilson tennis balls and a case of Henry's. A perfect combination.

Mickey had insisted on cooking the dinner now that she was feeling better. The main course was an elaborately produced dish she called Veal Oscar.

"I thought you didn't eat veal," I said. Mickey was into animal rights. The treatment of veal calves was one of her issues.

"I don't. That's tenderized beef. You won't notice the difference."

With the help of several bottles of Korbel champagne, we didn't.

After dinner Mickey poured us all snifters of cognac and we discussed the case.

"Good thing the doctors saved Clyde's life. For Barbara's sake," Mickey said.

"Yeah. I heard from Nancy today. She's hired a top-gun lawyer for Barbara. I give her every chance of getting off."

"What else did she say?"

"Thank you and the check's in the mail. And she said good-bye. She's going on a cruise to the South Pacific to get away from it all."

"A nice woman," the Chief said.

"Yes," I said softly, recalling the last time I had actually been alone with her. But I had no regrets.

As the Chief started to doze off. Mickey and I stared out at the white lights of the bridge and the bay.

I thought of some of the things that came together to lead us to Clyde. There was the molested little girl. She got me thinking and I remembered how much Jackie wanted to get away from home and her stepfather. My dealings with Jackie suggested that black-mail would be right up her alley. And if she and her mother stayed in touch, she had to know about the money Clyde inherited. It would be that perfect revenge she had talked about with Sherry Wine. Would all of this have come together if a Catholic priest had not gone on a rampage destroying condom machines in gay bars? Or if the Chief had not agreed to let the Archbishop handle the case discreetly? We would have never got the call that sent Mickey after Blummer, our first child abuser.

Or would it all have been revealed in a different way, layer by layer stripped off, like Salome in her dance of the seven veils? Of course, she got St. John's head on a platter from Herod for her performance. A fate I managed to avoid so far. The Seven Veils name had been a bad omen for everyone named Gutman and a lot of customers but not for me and my partners.

Mickey sipped her cognac. The Chief was fast asleep. The weary soldier.

It was strange. In his brutal way General Bloodhart had made some sense. But extorting money from the Vietnamese and merce-nary escapades was not the way to get our MIA's and POW's back. I had heard this living proof of their existence was getting our government interested in the issue again and that was good news. Now it would be out in the open instead of in the shadows of the CIA. Which had to be better.

I got up and looked at the lights on the Bay Bridge.

Tommy Dong was happy enough to send us a bonus that included $5,000 in chips good only at his poker houses. I was looking forward to a little action.

I had been afraid of a big loss on the Mendocino invasion but things had turned out well. I returned the tapes of Starborn's wife to him with a bill for expenses that included all of the vehicle rental charges, the cost of guns and ammunition and food supplies, and $250 a man for the Dragon Seeds and the Yellow Suns, and $15,000 for the Agency. A grand total that matched the amount in the briefcase. Perfectly reasonable, it seemed to me.

Reverend Starborn wasn't happy about it but I was holding the tapes of his wife's performance in one hand and my bill in the other.

He paid.

Hell, the Church of the Second Coming—Western Rite could well afford it. At least until the auditors got at the books of the TV ministry.

He gave me the torn-up briefcase which still contained the money. I didn't bother to count it.

He wished me an eternity in hell as I left.

My partners, who could never forget the money I had left behind in the Silverman case, had much nicer things to say. And a lot of suggestions on how to spend our share. Starting with bars on the upstairs windows.

"Now that the protection racket is broken, the Chews are going to cater a lunch for the Dragon Seeds and the Yellow Suns to express their gratitude. That's going to be a hell of a party," I said.

"Uh-huh," Mickey muttered. I knew she was fading.

I kissed Mickey on the forehead and went into the kitchen to clean up. When I was done, Mickey was sound asleep leaning on the Chief. I woke him and whispered, "Let's go."

We got out without Mickey so much as stirring.

25

Our ballplayer client, Pete, came through with four box seat tickets to the A's-Yankees game on Memorial Day at the Oakland Coliseum. The game was scheduled to start at six-fifteen to allow time for a fireworks display when it was over. We got there early because the Chief drove like he was on the warpath against all traffic. He had added a cover to the back of his pickup truck and some uncomfortable items that he claimed were seats. He and Mickey rode in front and Curtis and I in the back. It wasn't a hell of a lot of fun.

Curtis, who was wearing an old Giants baseball cap, hadn't seen a baseball game since he got back from Vietnam. First thing we did after buying him a program was to buy him a new A's hat. He looked at it funny but put it on.

Our field level box seats were right by the A's dugout.

"Nice seats. How'd you get 'em?" Curtis asked.

"We helped a ballplayer. The kid playing left field tonight," Mickey explained.

The Chief and I went to get ball-park dinners for everyone. We took orders and came back with two cardboard trays filled with jumbo hot dogs, Italian sausage dogs, Cajun dogs, and Polish dogs. I made a separate trip back for sixteen-ounce cups of Bud.

The Chief applauded my beer selection.

"Limited choices here, Chief," I explained.

We had settled into our seats with dinner just in time to have to get up for a black soul singer belting out the National Anthem.

The first two innings were routine for the pitchers. No one reached first base. We got through the meal.

There was no score by the fourth inning. The lights had been on since the start of the game and now it was growing cold. I didn't have a silky jacket like the Chief's but at least I had a London Fog windbreaker. Curtis had nothing but a thin T-shirt.

When he got up to use the rest room, I went and bought him an A's warmup jacket.

"Oh, man." he said as he put it on. "Why'd you do that?"

"A bonus. For all the help you've been. And it goes with the hat."

Curtis blinked his eyes. "Shee-it. That ain't what I mean. I'm a Giants fan."

I went to get us another round of Bud. When I got back, I asked Curtis, "How are those MIA's doing?" A few of them were staying at the Dragon Seeds headquarters now that the army was through debriefing them. I had heard that the army and the CIA were interested in talking to me, too, but so far nothing. Most likely they were just going to bury the Bloodhart fiasco.

"Not bad. They glad to be free a the Gen'ral. But they still talk 'bout their buddies over there. Some of 'em really wanted to go."

"Think these guys will make it here?" I asked.

"A couple headed back to the hills. Some are in VA hospitals. An we got a lot of 'em just gone back to their families."

"I wish them luck."

"So do I," Curtis said.

There wasn't much action in this game. Pete was doing all right but no one else was doing much. This had to go down as a boring game or a pitchers' duel.

I went to get us the last beers of the night. We paid attention to the responsible drinking signs posted all over the ball park. Besides, the vendors didn't sell beer after the seventh inning.

By the eighth inning, the A's were ahead by a run. I noticed Mickey grinning at me. It was probably that third beer. But she didn't stop.

"What's so funny?" I asked.

"I went out for lunch with Dr. Koyota yesterday. He took me to the Cliff House."

"So?" Mr. Cool.

"I showed him where I was shot."

"What? Why?" I sputtered.

"He asked."

"Eagle eye, what can you see from the Cliff House?" the Chief asked.

"Huh?"

"The Dutch Windmill," Curtis answered.

"Where I was shot," Mickey concluded.

Everybody looked at me. I laughed harder than anyone.

After the game there was a spectacular fireworks display that reminded Curtis of mortar attacks in Vietnam. We decided not to stay. As we went toward the parking lot showers of red, white, and blue exploded overhead.

Curtis stopped and looked up. "Ain't so bad," he said.

We sat on the hood of the Chief's truck and watched the rest of the Memorial Day show in silence. I thought of my father buried in D.C. This was his day. Which doesn't mean a hell of a lot if you're dead. When it was over, we were the first ones out of the parking lot. The Chief didn't like waiting in line. Ever.

We dropped Curtis off in the Tenderloin, then the Chief drove to Mickey's. I told the Chief to wait and walked her to the door. Dr. Earnhard and his toupee were out of the picture. He was going to remarry his fourth ex-wife, the beautiful blond Gloria, my sexy tennis partner. It had all been announced on his TV spot.

Earnhard aside, I knew I had to take it slow. "Good night, partner," I said and kissed her on the cheek. She kissed me back and went inside. The Chief drove me home.